JN034236

ロシア海軍少尉 《ゴローウニン事件》

徳川幕府に囚われたムールの獄中上申書

ムールの苦悩

日本語版 岩 下 哲 典

英語版 アンナ リネア・カーランデル 共著

●右文書院●

本書をムールと村上貞助に捧げる

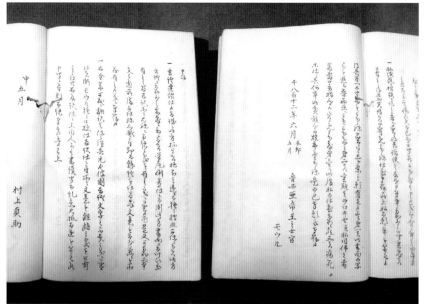

(右)1812年6月魯西亜帝王の士官モウルと記載されている
(左)村上貞助はゴローウニン事件のロシア語通詞

「模烏児獄中上表　上下」(明海大学図書館〈所蔵〉)

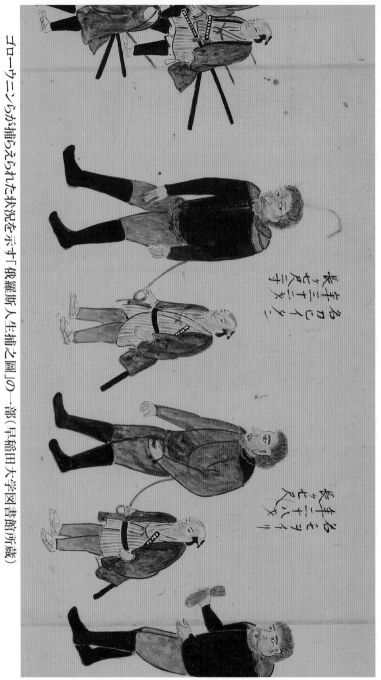

ゴローウニンらが捕らえられた状況を示す「俄羅斯人生捕之圖」の一部（早稲田大学図書館所蔵）
「カビイタン」はゴローウニン、「モヲイリ」はムールである。

（図中の書き込み）
長ケ三尺二寸
名ヲ ビイトル

長手ヶ三尺二寸
名ヲ ビイトリ

目次

凡例

1. 本書は、19世紀初頭に日本の国後島に来航し、期せずして日本側に捕縛・幽閉されたロシア帝国海軍士官フョードル・フョードロヴィチ・ムールの獄中上申書である。

　なお、同時に捕縛・幽閉されたもののなかに、ヴァシーリー・ミハイロヴィチ・ゴローウニンがいた。帰国後、ゴローウニンは『日本幽囚記』を執筆刊行したが、ムールの上申書のほうは残念ながら刊行されなかった。

2. 現在、ムールによりロシア語で書かれた原本は、その存在が確認されていない。

3. ロシア語原本から日本人ロシア語通詞村上貞助が翻訳した江戸時代の日本語による写本が、北海道大学、函館市立函館図書館、明海大学、早稲田大学、国立公文書館、国立国会図書館、名古屋市蓬左文庫、国際日本文化研究センター等に所蔵されている。

4. その中でも比較的良質の写本が、明海大学メディアセンター（図書館）所蔵の「模鳥児獄中上表」（1冊）である。以下、明海本と呼ぶ。

5. 本書は、まず明海本の本文を岩下哲典が、現代日本語の文字に置き換えた釈文（しゃくもん・江戸時代日本語文）を作成した。岩下が釈文を現代日本語に翻訳し、本書に収録した。その現代日本語文をアンナ・カーランダーが現代英語に翻訳して同じく本書に収録した。

6. 凡例・解説・あとがき・付記も岩下がそれを英語文に翻訳した。なお、日本語文の解説は、『洋学史研究』第31号、2014年に掲載した拙文を若干の字句の修正を行い収録したが、英語文においては註は訳出していない。

7. 本書の構成は、凡例、解説、上申書本文、あとがき、付記とし、それぞれ日本語文の部分と英語文のそれとした。

8. 日本語文の「訳註」はロシア語通詞村上貞助のものである。

ゴローウニン事件とナポレオン情報

――わが国におけるナポレオン情報の嚆矢「ムール獄中上申書」――

はじめに

本稿[1]の目的は、ゴローウニン事件が、ナポレオン情報とどのような関係があるのか詳述することである。

その前に江戸時代における徳川幕府の海外情報の管理の実態に関して簡単に概観しておくこととする。

今日、17世紀中葉から19世紀の、つまり「開港・開市」以前の徳川幕府の対外関係は、いわゆる「鎖国」という言葉で表現されている。しかし、その言葉は、19世紀になって、来日ドイツ人ケンペルの表現を日本人が翻訳造語したものである[2]。かつ、その言葉の持つ意味は、実はかなり複雑な様相を呈していて、実態は多岐にわたる。

思うに近世の対外関係の眼目、つまり為政者の最大の関心は、体制を揺るがしかねないキリ

スト教の禁令（一六一二）であることは論を俟たない。キリスト教の流入を防ぐには、海外からの人・物・情報の管理・統制を十分に行う必要があった。そのために、以下の政策が矢継ぎ早にとられたと言ってよいだろう。

すなわち、長崎奉行を設置し長崎を直轄地化した（一六三三）。そのうえで、日本人の海外渡航を禁止し（一六三五）、ポルトガル船の来航も禁止した（一六三九）。加えてオランダ人を出島に軟禁状態にし（一六四一）、幕府直営貿易は長崎に限定、それも唐（中国）・蘭（オランダ）のみとした。これにより海外情報はオランダと中国に多くを依存する体制ができあがった（そのほかには偶然漂着した異国人からの情報、偶然にも帰国できた漂流民の情報があった）。長崎（港）の防衛は、福岡・佐賀・大村藩の軍役として担当させた。一方、幕府は対アイヌ民族交易は松前藩（一六〇四）に、対朝鮮王国応接は対馬藩（一六〇七〜）に、対琉球王国応接は薩摩藩（一六〇九、一六三四〜）に担当させた。また、寛永期には、海岸防備と通報システムを全国に張り巡らし、オランダ人には、その忠節の証として、定期的な海外情報たるオランダ風説書を提出させた（一六四四〜、但し制度化は一六五九）[3]。こうして、実態としてのいわゆる「鎖国」が成立したのである。ただし、近年、中国の海禁政策の研究成果をもとに「海禁」と呼ぶこともある[4]。ただこの用語も、使用されたのは近世後期で家光時代からの対外関係を直接示す言葉ではない。現時点での私見では便宜的に、「いわゆる『鎖国』」と呼ぶのが近世日本の対

外関係を述べる際には適当ではないかと考える。

1. ゴローウニン事件と「ムール獄中上申書」

先に記した通り、徳川幕府の対外関係、いわゆる「鎖国」は、外交文書・使節の交換関係にある「通信の国」としての琉球・朝鮮と直轄貿易を行う「通商の国」としての中国（明・清）とオランダに限定されていた。ところが、16世紀後半にロシアが極東に進出しはじめ[5]、18世紀中葉には日本近海にデンマーク出身士官マルチン・ペトローヴィチ・シパンベルク（ロシア名。デンマーク名：モルチン・スパンベア）指揮のロシア軍艦が出没し[6]、18世紀末には「開港・開市」（通商）を求めるロシア使節ラクスマンの根室来航があった[7]。さらに19世紀初頭には同じくロシアのレザーノフの長崎来航と幕府の拒絶にあって、レザーノフの部下が腹いせのように行った蝦夷地襲撃[8]によって、徳川幕府は北方への警戒を強めていた。すなわち、幕府直轄たる蝦夷地では、ロシアの来襲に備え最高度の警戒態勢をとっていたのである。

1811年、北太平洋の測量のため、日本に接近しつつあったロシア海軍ディアナ号艦長ゴローウニンは、そうとは知らず、国後島に小人数で上陸したところを幕府側に捕縛され、松前に監禁された[9]。ディアナ号に残った副艦長リコルドは報復措置として、幕府御用商人高田屋嘉兵衛を捕え、のちには双方の人質交換が成立して、1813年この一件は決着した。これに

よりロシア人は約束を守る、よき隣人との印象を幕府に与えたのである。なお、現代の日本で
このように考える日本人は少ないのが実情である。

さらにこの時、ゴローウニンとともに監禁された一行の中にムール少尉というロシア軍人がいた。松前に監禁された直後の1812年にゴローウニンらは脱獄を図るが、ムールだけは脱獄しなかった。絵心があったムールは、その描く絵を通して日本人と良好なコミュニケーションをとることができるようになり、日本に帰化して日本政府（幕府）の西洋言語通訳として働きたいとの希望を持つに至ったのである[10]。

なお、これは長島要一氏のいう「文化の翻訳」[11] 状態のごく初期の状態がムールに生じたのではないかと分析できる。すなわち、長島氏によれば「文化の翻訳」は「世界を『他者』の目で見ることの出来る能力、自分の文化的背景を他者のそれに照射して、自他の文化の総体を俯瞰できるバイカルチャル（二つの文化を身に付けた状態や二つの文化を身に付けること――引用者註）の能力」とされる。

ムールが、日本とロシアの、双方の文化の総体を俯瞰できたかどうかは不明ながら、少なくとも日本に友好的な心情を覚え、日本に帰化して日本政府のために外国語（主に西洋言語）の通訳になるためには、ロシアを相対的に見て、ロシア国家からの離脱を考えたわけで、自らの出身母体であるロシア自体を相対的にみていたことを示している。おそらく、そうした「文化

6

の翻訳」状態がムールに生じつつあったと考える。

ともかくムールはゴローウニンと同一の行動（脱獄）をとらなかったのである。おそらくムールは史上初の日本帰化を熱望したロシア人として特筆されるべき人物である。ところで、獄中に残ったムールは、のちに「ムール獄中上申書」と名づけられる、日露関係史上のみならず、日本における対外関係史上重要な資料を作成した。ロシア語で書かれた上申書は、ロシア語通詞村上貞助らによって日本語に翻訳され、松前奉行を経由して幕府老中に上申された[12]。

上申書の内容は、それを書くに至った心情、レザーノフの長崎来航、ゴローウニンの職務とその活動、レザーノフの部下フボストフの蝦夷地襲撃、ゴローウニンの脱獄事件、ロシア国情、ヨーロッパおよびナポレオン情報である。いずれも当時の幕府にとって非常に重要な情報であるが、ここでは特に近世日本にとって重大なナポレオン情報に関して述べておく。

実は文献上最初のナポレオン情報は、この「ムールの獄中上申書」なのである。これまで、1813年に日本にもたらされたロシア語新聞のナポレオンの記事が最初といわれていたが、1812年のこの上申書が、文献上、現在知られる最も古いナポレオン情報である。つまりオランダ商館が、ナポレオンをひた隠しに隠したため、ナポレオン情報は南の長崎ではなく北の蝦夷地、それも偶然に捕縛されたゴローウニン一行からもたらされたのである。そして、リコルドがもたらした前述のロシア語新聞に、オランダの首都であったアムステルダムがナポレオ

ンの勅令によりナポレオン帝国の第三の都市になったと書かれていたことから、長崎出島のオランダ商館に真偽の程が問い合わされた。

それに対する長崎のオランダ人の言い訳がふるっている。

「その通報はまだ接していないが十分にありえることである。」[13]

実のところ、オランダ商館はフランスによるオランダ併合という事実を知りつつ隠蔽していたのだが、こういわれても幕府には確かめるすべはなかった。やはり西洋関係の情報ルートが一つでは限界があったのだ。

2. ヨーロッパにおける幕府天文方の「ムール獄中上申書」出版計画

しかしながら、当時、幕府における最高水準の西洋学術・知識の調査研究機関であった、天文方（本来は暦や各種地図を作製する機関）は新たな展開を考えていたことは刮目に価する[14]。

1816年、ゴローウニンがロシアで『日本幽囚記』を刊行した。これがオランダ経由で長崎から幕府天文方にもたらされた。1825年、早速天文方でオランダ語版を翻訳したところ、「ムール獄中上申書」と相違する箇所がいくつも見つかったのである。ムールは日本に友好的な心情をもって上申書を作成したが、ゴローウニンはそうではなかったこともあろう。ムールの方を先に読んでいた天文方は、ゴローウニンの言は正しくないと考えたと思われる。そして、

8

「ムール獄中上申書」の諸本を収集し、定本を確定して、それをオランダ語に翻訳し、さらに版を計画した。ムールとゴローウニン、どちらが正しいか、ヨーロッパの人々に判断してもらおうと考えていた。(15)この計画の推進者であった書物奉行兼天文方高橋景保が、1828年のシーボルト事件で失脚しなければ、実現していたかもしれない。高橋があれほどシーボルトに肩入れしたのは、シーボルトを介して、アムステルダムでの出版を実現したかったからかもしれない。高橋のもともとの思惑は、もちろんヨーロッパ情報を入手することにもあったが、逆に、日本発の情報をヨーロッパで発信する意図もあったのではないかと考えている。そうであれば、これなどは、実に高度な、幕府一部機関の情報収集活動と言ってよいだろう。情報を収集するだけでなく情報を発信してヨーロッパの世論を変えようという画期的な企画である。こうしたことを構想した江戸人がいたことを私たちは誇りに思うべきであろう。

ただし、こうしたことは、実はひとり天文方だけではなく、蘭学者たちも考えていたことである。たとえば1774年の「解体新書」訳述も、漢文で書かれたのは、日本のみならず、漢字文化圏、特に中国において読まれることを想定していたと言われる。(16)それゆえに現在でも中国の医学用語の中には日本経由のものもあるという。(17)また、幕府医官桂川甫賢は、東洋で最古の国際学会バタビア芸術科学協会の会員にも推薦されている。(18)こうなると、もはや、い

9　2．ヨーロッパにおける幕府天文方の「ムール獄中上申書」出版計画

わゆる「鎖国」は、天文方や蘭学者の願いとは相容れないものとなっていく。つまり日本の行く末を思えば思うほど、その時点でさらなる情報収集活動を阻んでいる、いわゆる「鎖国」は足枷以外の何物でもない。それが変わらない以上、情報収集活動は隠密的なものにならざるを得ない。ところが時として蘭学者の情報収集活動が、幕府に不穏な動きとして発覚・指弾される。1828年のシーボルト事件、1839年の蛮社の獄はその顕著な事例である。これらの事件は、蘭学者の活動を委縮させるように見えた。

3．ゴローウニン事件以後のナポレオン情報

　ところで、天文方の高橋景保は、江戸参府するオランダ商館長の服装の変化からヨーロッパ情勢の変転を察知し、ナポレオン情報をも収集した。[19] その結果が、1826年の「丙戌異聞（へいじゅういぶん）」「別埒阿利安設戦記（べれありあんせっせんき）」だった。前者は、ナポレオンの簡単な伝記、後者はワーテルローの戦いに特化した戦記である。しかし、景保がシーボルト事件で獄死したため、その研究は、岸和田藩医で幕府天文方蕃書和解御用に任命された小関三英（こせきさんえい）に受け継がれた。

　三英は景保の仕事を批判的に継承し、略伝である「卜那把盧的略伝（ボナパルテ）」（1829年ごろ）、さらに1832年から蛮社の獄で自殺する1839年までに「那波列翁伝（ナポレオン）」を翻訳した。特に後者は、アミアンの和約までで終わっており、ナポレオンの伝記としては中途であるが、フラン

10

ス革命への言及もあり、またナポレオンの伝記としては江戸時代もっとも詳しいものである。

後に浜松藩医牧穆中や津山藩医箕作阮甫は、これに刺激を受けさらに充実したナポレオンの伝記完成を目指した。また、田原藩士松岡与権は三英による伝記を1857年に刊行し、さらにそれらを読んだ松代藩儒佐久間象山、長州藩士吉田松陰はナポレオンに関する漢詩を作り、薩摩藩士西郷隆盛は自らとナポレオンを重ねるなど、幕末の志士に大きな影響を及ぼした。

ほかにも古河藩家老鷹見泉石は、イタリア戦役の銅版画、鉛製の兵隊人形やネルソン記念小物入れなどオランダ渡りのナポレオン関連グッズを蒐集し、さらにはオランダ一国のみの詳細な地図を作製しているが、これもナポレオン情報が及ぼした影響と言えるだろう。なお、泉石は、1853年のペリー来航に際しての意見書「愚意摘要」の中でロシア船渡来に言及し、「同十年九月『コロウィン』『モウル』其外之迎船江御戻し」[20]と記述している。泉石の海外情報の背景の一つにゴローウニン事件における「ムール嶽中上申書」があったことをうかがわせる記述をしていることは重要である。実際、古河歴史博物館所蔵鷹見家資料の中には「ムール嶽中上申書」等の写本があり、[21]それらは泉石の旧蔵本と思われる。

そのほか、最幕末の1867年には、福地源一郎が「那破倫兵法」を著した。これは、来るべき戊辰の実戦に備えたものと考えられる。

1867年、最後の将軍徳川慶喜は、いわゆる「大政奉還」の建白書（正確には「政権奉帰」

の建白書)を朝廷に提出した。この時点ではまだ政権を返すと言っているだけで、完全に返したのではない。慶喜が目指したのは、ナポレオン帝国であり、自らがナポレオンになることだった。しかし、王政復古、天皇親政が決定的になって、慶喜のもくろみは大きく外れた。ナポレオンになったのは明治天皇だったのである。

それでも、幕府陸軍のフランス軍事顧問団ジュール・ブリュネらは、榎本武揚らと箱館まで転戦し、「四稜郭」を構築する指導までした。フランス士官は、旧幕府軍の中にいた親フランス派に共鳴していたのである。そして驚くべきことに明治政府は一八八二年と一八九五年、ブリュネに勲章を授与している。明治政府の中にも親フランス派はいたのである。これは幕府や明治政府を問わず、ナポレオン情報が当時の日本人にいかに広く読まれたかを示しており、ナポレオン情報が近世後期、幕末維新、明治と求められた証左なのである。

ナポレオンは、一八二一年にセントヘレナ島で死んだが、四七年後の戊辰戦争でも、七〇年後の日清戦争でも、忘れられずに日本人の心の中に生きていたのである。

　おわりに

　江戸後期から幕末維新期の日本において、ナポレオン情報が果たした役割や意義を述べてきた。まず、日本にもたらされた最初のナポレオン情報が、19世紀初期のゴローウニン事件のさ

なかであり、ゴローウニン一行の中にいたロシア軍人ムールの獄中上申書であったことを指摘した。さらにこのナポレオン情報が、当時最高の西洋事情研究機関であった幕府天文方に与えた影響は大きく、またその天文方がオランダ商館あるいはオランダ人等を通じてアムステルダムなどヨーロッパでなそうとした、獄中上申書出版計画とその結果に関して述べた。そして、その後、天文方は幕府当局からの政治的弾圧によって萎縮を余儀なくさせられ、ナポレオン研究は一蘭学者、すなわち小関三英の手によってなされたこと、彼の著作が、佐久間象山、吉田松陰や西郷隆盛などに及ぼした影響に関して言及した。また、鷹見泉石や徳川慶喜とナポレオンの関係についても述べた。全体としてナポレオン情報が、江戸後期や幕末の日本にどのような衝撃を与えたのかを概括できた。最後に、幕府内部や明治政府内の親フランス派とフランス軍事顧問団についても言及した。

これらから総括すると、ナポレオン情報の伝達と拡散に関してはゴローウニン事件と「ムール獄中上申書」が非常に重要であることが指摘できる[26]。すなわち、わが国がナポレオン情報を入手し得たもっとも早い時期のものでもあり、従来海外情報の入手先として重要だと考えられた長崎ではなく、北方から入手した重要情報である点、また幕府情報機関がヨーロッパで刊行しようとしたことからも、特筆すべき事例ということができるのである。

註

（1）本稿に関係する岩下の著作は以下の通り。①「開国前後の日本における西洋英雄伝とその受容」「洋学史研究」第10号、1993年）、②『江戸のナポレオン伝説』［中公新書、1999年］、③『江戸の海外情報ネットワーク』［吉川弘文館、2006年］、④「江戸時代における日露関係史上の主要事件に関する史料について」［竹内誠監修『外国人が見た近世日本』角川学芸出版、2009年］、⑤「一八世紀～一九世紀初頭における露・英の接近と近世日本の変容」［笠谷和比古編『一八世紀日本の文化状況と国際環境』思文閣出版、2011年］。

なお、ナポレオンの受容史研究は、最初に青山学院大学に卒業論文として提出し、それを学術論文として①「開国前後の日本における西洋英雄伝とその受容」を発表した。その後、それをもとに②の『江戸のナポレオン伝説』で一般向けに概説したが、新知見を多く盛り込んだ。さらに、③『江戸の海外情報ネットワーク』や④「江戸時代における日露関係史上の主要事件に関する史料について」で拡充してきた。それらを勘案して⑤「一八世紀～一九世紀初頭における露・英の接近と近世日本の変容」を作成した。特に本論文と関係が深いのは②③④である。さらに、ムールやゴローウニンに関する人物情報は岩下編『江戸時代来日外国人人名辞典』［東京堂出版、2011年］を参照されたい。

（2）大島明秀『「鎖国」という言説―ケンペル著・志筑忠雄訳「鎖国論」の受容史』［ミネルヴァ書房、2009年］参照。

（3）松方冬子『オランダ風説書と近世日本』［東京大学出版会、2007年］、同『オランダ風説書』［中公新書、

14

（4）荒野泰典『近世日本と東アジア』［東京大学出版会、一九八八年］、同「海禁・華夷秩序体制の形成」『「地球的世界の成立」（日本の対外関係5）吉川弘文館、二〇一三年］参照。

（5）ロシア南下の実態は、秋月俊幸『日本北辺の探検と地図の歴史』［北海道大学図書刊行会、一九九九年］および平川新『開国への道』（日本の歴史・江戸時代・19世紀）小学館、二〇〇八年］が詳しい。なおこの近世後期の対外関係に関しては、藤田覚『近世後期政治史と対外関係』［東京大学出版会、二〇〇五年］参照。また以下の研究も参照した。郡山良光『幕末日露関係史研究』［国書刊行会、一九八〇年］、大熊良一『幕末北方関係史考』［近藤出版社、一九九〇年］、木村汎『日露国境交渉史』［中央公論新社、一九九三年］。

（6）長島要一『日本デンマーク交流史 一六〇〇—一八七三』［東海大学出版会、二〇〇七年］。なお註（1）『江戸時代来日外国人人名辞典』も参照。

（7）木崎良平『光太夫とラクスマン』［刀水書房、一九九二年］および生田美智子『外交儀礼から見た幕末日露文化交流史』［ミネルヴァ書房、一九九九年］参照。

（8）木崎良平『仙台漂民とレザノフ』［刀水書房、一九九七年］および松本英治「19世紀はじめの日露関係とオランダ商館」『開国以前の日露関係』東北大学東北アジア研究センター、二〇〇六年］参照。

（9）真鍋重忠『日露関係史』［吉川弘文館、一九七八年］参照。以下、同書による。

（10）「ムール獄中上申書」の写本のひとつ「魯西亜人モウル存寄書」（国際日本文化研究センター所蔵）および『日

二〇一〇年］参照。

本幽囚記（上・中・下）、［岩波文庫、一九四三～四六年］参照。

⑾　長島要一『「文化の翻訳」と先駆者森鷗外』『鷗外』第88号、二〇一一年］参照。

⑿　前掲註⑴④「江戸時代における日露関係史上の主要事件に関する史料について」参照。以下論文によると
ころが大きい。

⒀　前掲註⑴②『江戸のナポレオン伝説』参照。以下、同書による。

⒁　前掲註⑴③『江戸の海外情報ネットワーク』参照。以下同書による。

⒂　註⑽『魯西亜人モウル存寄書』では「ゴローウニンは新都に帰りて爵一級を陞せられ、躬其始末を詳記し遭
厄日本紀事二策を著せり、予去年紀事和訳浄書の旨を蒙り其の書を反復するにゴローウニン彼か出奔の儀に
加はらさるを恨みモールを反賊たりと記し誹謗すること甚し、今此書を視るにモール豈反賊ならんや、ゴロー
ウニンか徒のモールの訴に従はさりしこと惜しむべけれ、実にゴローウニンか出奔せしは己か誤にして魯西
亜王国の恥辱と謂ふべし、而ゴローウニンたとひモールか異見には従はさりしを愉すとも豈に己か非を悟り
死セしモールを罟り記するに忍ぶべけんや、夷情黙恨悪むへきのミ、此書ことくモールか願の如く魯西亜人
の手に入らは、孰か是孰か非百年の後必長嘆息するものあらん」と記されている。また同書には全編に亘り
諸本との校訂が施されており、定本を確定しようとしていたことが明らかである。本史料に関しては、松田
清『洋学の書誌的研究』［臨川書店、一九九八年］参照。

⒃　片桐一男『杉田玄白』（人物叢書新装版）［吉川弘文館、一九八六年］参照。

(17)村田和美『神経』第二の意味の派生および日中における影響関係について」『明海大学大学院応用言語学研究科紀要』第10号、2008年」参照。

(18)石山禎一「桂川甫賢」『洋学史事典』[雄松堂出版、1984年]参照。

(19)また、ドベルク・美那子『高橋景保とJ・W・ド・ストゥルレル』『日蘭学会会誌』第31号、2006年参照。また、註(1)①『開国前後の日本における西洋英雄伝とその受容』および②『江戸のナポレオン伝説』参照。以下、同書による。

(20)片桐一男『鷹見泉石の蘭学攷究』『大倉山論集』第11号、1974年」参照。なお鷹見泉石の最新の研究は、同『蘭学家老鷹見泉石の来翰を読む―蘭学篇―』[鷹見本雄、2013年]および同『鷹見泉石』[中央公論新社、2019年]である。

(21)「『魯西亜人ガワビン外五人出奔吟味書付等留書』」が当該資料と思われる。

(22)岩下哲典『高邁なる幕臣 高橋泥舟』[教育評論社、2012年]参照。

(23)明治政府が作ろうとした明治天皇のイメージは武人的天皇であるが、そのイメージの源流はナポレオンであろうと思われる。これに関しては、拙著『江戸将軍が見た地球』メディアファクトリー、2011年で少し触れたことがある。

(24)片山宏「ジュール・ブリュネと大鳥圭介」[片桐一男編『日蘭交流史 その人・物・情報』思文閣出版、2002年」参照。

(25)澤護『お雇いフランス人の研究』[敬愛大学経済文化研究所、一九九一年]参照。

(26)コペンハーゲン大学でのシンポジウムでは、今後の課題として以下の事を最後に述べた（要旨）。

今後は、「ムール獄中上表」を英訳して、ゴローウニンの『日本幽囚記』とは別の視覚をもった日本研究資料をヨーロッパやロシアの方々に提供したいと思う。　特に日本に帰化を希望したロシア人の事績は、最高に冷え切った今日の日露両国の外交関係に一筋の光明となろう。　なおムールの存在を今に伝える遺物として、ライフル自殺をしたムールのためにゴローウニンが自身が『日本幽囚記』の中で述べている通り、ペトロパブロフスク・カムチャツキーに建てた墓石があるらしい。　しかしながら、いまだに誰も確認したことがない。　これもぜひ現地で確認したいと思う。　いずれにしても、「ムール獄中上表」のもっとも重要な写本が国際日本文化研究センター（日文研）に所蔵されており、それを日文研が主催する海外シンポジウム、それもロシアに距離的に近い北欧で紹介できたことは大変ありがたく思う。　考えてみるとムールの思いを二〇〇年ぶりに紹介できたことになる。　シンポジウム開催に尽力された、長島要一先生、佐野真由子先生に感謝申し上げる。

付記

本稿は、二〇一二年八月にデンマークのコペンハーゲン大学で行われた、国際日本文化研究センター主催シンポジウム「日本再考」に「幕末日本とナポレオン情報」と題して研究発表を行い、さらに二〇一三年一月の

洋学史研究会新春研究集会で「ゴローウニン事件と『ムール獄中上表』」として研究発表したものを、その後の知見を取り込み、大巾に改稿したものである。なお、シンポジウムの成果は、岩下哲典「幕末日本とナポレオン情報」『Rethinking "Japanese Studies" from Practices in the Nordic Region 日本研究再考—北欧の実践から（北欧シンポジウム2012）』国際日本文化研究センター、2014年（シンポジウム参加者に配布された限定本）として刊行されている。特に、洋学史研究会新春研究大会では、片桐一男先生をはじめ諸先生方から大変有益なご助言を頂いた。さらに成稿に際しては、片桐先生からたいへんご懇切なご指導を賜った。ほかにも、松本英治氏より御尽力を賜った。記してお礼申し上げる。

（本稿の初出は洋学史研究会編集・発行『洋学史研究』第31号、2014年である）

19世紀初頭の日本で幽閉されたロシア士官ムールによる獄中からの上申書　上下

原著者　フョードル・フョードロヴィチ・ムール

江戸時代日本語翻訳者　村上貞助

現代日本語翻訳者　岩下哲典

現代英語翻訳者　Anna Linnea Carlander

ムールによる獄中からの上申書　上下

ロシア人ムールが書き上げた西洋文字の文面を翻訳した書である

考えを申上げた文面

大日本帝王〔岩下註：征夷大将軍〕の地方軍隊駐屯地である松前ならびに国後・択捉そのほか

の場所の御奉行小笠原伊勢守・荒尾但馬守様へ

1.　ロシア帝国皇帝の士官であるムールが謹んで申し上げます。

　御奉行所は、去年以来、大きなお考えでもって親切なご対応をしてくださいました。私たちは日夜忘れがたく、いずれ国王の面前に出ることもあり得ますので、その時は、いただきました御恩の数々を申し述べたいと思います。また私たちは御役人方々のご健康を心よりお祈りいたしますとともに、今回のことは永く忘れずにいたいと思います。

　この度、思いがけず同伴の者が悪心をもち、ご厚恩を軽んじて逃亡したことは、私や遭難したロシア人にとって再び暗中に投げ入れられたことになり、以前のような楽しいことなどもすべてなくなってしまったと思いました。しかしながら、御奉行所においては、御慈悲をもって逃亡した者の心の中をお察しくださり、御咎めもなく、ますますのご憐憫のお諭しをいただきました。もはや帰国が絶望となったうえは、ご厚恩に報いることが出来なければ、かえって心苦しく思います。かつ日々、士道や宗旨も変化し、才智も次第に減っていくように感じるばかりでございます。どこで、私は無駄な時を過ごして良いものでしょうか。ただ、御奉行所からいただきましたご厚恩の万分の一でもお報いしたいと、私の心中にありますことなど残すところなく申し上げたいと思います。

私どもロシアの法では異国人がロシアを憎んだり恥辱を与えたりすることは厳しく禁じられています。かつ、ご当国〔岩下註：日本〕の習俗では外国に対して実に疑念が強く、私どもに限らず、ヨーロッパ諸国の航海者には理解ができないことであります。日本人の話では「岩礁や砂州多き海中を航海するのは遭難するのを自分から望むこと」ということわざもあります。こうしたことからこれまでは何事も申上げないできました。

2.

私どもはこれまで日本に来たことがありませんでした。択捉島に上陸して初めて日本に所属する島だということが理解できました。ただし御役人に面通しがあった際、その時はだれもそのことを申上げませんでしたので、御役人はかえって安心されたのではないかと思います。さまざまに御教示またお手紙までいただきましたが、食料はだんだん差支え、いろいろやむを得ないことなど御教えに従い、欺瞞をなさないよう心掛けて、いろいろ言わないようにしていました。しかしながら、悪心を持った者は何事にもはかりごとを構えてしまいますが、悪心を抱かないものは自分の心に引き当て、他人も悪心を抱かないと心得て、そのように承知していました。その結果、このような御厄介になることに立ち入りました。そうしたところ、箱館においてお尋ねの時、盗賊を行うために来日したのかと、

3.

それとも戦争をするために来日したのか尋問されましたが、それぞれ理由がございました。エレザノフ〔訳註：このエレザノフという者は長崎にやって来たレザノットである。今回文字

を翻訳したところエレザノフと表記していたので、その通り翻訳した〕へしかと伝達された、「この以後、ロシア船が来日した場合は、すべて焼き捨てる」の旨、私どもは初めて知ったことでありまして、まったく雷に打たれたようでございましたし、もはや本国へ帰還することもできないものと考えました。またフボストフの乱暴一件の始末を聞かされ、逐一お尋ねになられましたが、もとより他人の仕業で、私の知らないことであり、かつどのようなことを根拠に申し上げたらいいのか、逐一申し上げるべきことなのか、しかしながらこのことはいささか知っていることもありますが、十分に申し上げるべきことも知らないものです。

要するに、クリル諸島の異国人〔岩下註：後出のラショワ人のこと。キリスト教を受容し、ロシア化した千島アイヌ〕がすべて自分の利益をむさぼるために択捉に来るようになっていたため、ロシア本国の役人イスホラウニカ〔役名〕・ロマキン〔姓名〕という者から、蝦夷島（北海道）の様子を見てくるように言われ、そのため本国から船を出しました。松前には4艘、モハナイ〔訳註：モハナイは択捉・国後・色丹の三島より松前までのロシア側表記のようである。先住民族は髭がたくさんあるので、そのような名前になったといわれる〕へは3艘差し向けました。戦争をするなどという考えはまったく跡形もないこととのみと嘘偽りを申上げ、すべて日本側の意向に沿うことのみを申し上げたほうがよいということは私たちは入牢以後に知ったことでございます。船中にて聞いたことでは、ただ交易のために派

4.

　先だって御奉行所の御慈悲を以て、私どもの始末を書き上げるように命じられました。
そこで願書幷上申書を提出いたしました。そのうち申上げなかったことがらがありますが、

遣されたのだということだけで、このように前後左右から虚偽を以て私どもを難儀の中に
引き入れたのでございます。かつ、かねてお聞きしていた通り日本の習俗でお疑いの心多
く、私どもはどのように釈明するか難しかったのでございます。これらによりこれまでは
なかなか申し上げることができなかったことも多くございました。

　島異国人とは2年前、択捉島にやって来たラショワ人のことで、ロシア船が数艘松前幷択捉周辺
にやって来たとき、ラショワ人たちがその（ロシア人は来たことがないとの）ように申し立てた
とのこと。箱館の牢中でアレクセイが初めてムールに話したという。その時アレクセイが言うに
は、皆跡形もなく、すべて偽りのことで、私たち一人のほか偽りを申し上げたけれども、そうす
ればわれらの内一人だけが心悪いのだと御役人が理解し、他の者は帰島を命じられるのではない
かと思われ、自分たちのうち一人は帰島がかなわないことになるが、やむを得ずほかの者が申し
上げた通り、相違ないと申し立てたという。これらのことはムールに話したが、ムールが考えた
ところでは、たとえ偽りであっても、このようなことを申し立てたら、すべて日本御役人の御意
にかなうとのこと。このことは国後にてラショワ人どもが再審の節に申し立てたことと、同所詰
の支配向きのものが言うことと一致している〔訳註：本文のクリル諸

偽りを申し上げたことはありません。現在もそのように思っています。たとえこののちロシア本国の役人がこれらの書面を見ても、相違することはなく、日本の習俗を十分知っているので、私どもが悪心がなくても、このような難儀に遭遇したことも察してくれるものと思っています。

5. 御奉行所が私どもの心中を推察してくださりありがたく思います。この度書き上げました明細書には、私の臨終の節、生涯のことを懺悔する心づもりですから、ただ御奉行所だけでご覧いただきたく存じます。またこれまでお疑いのことも解けるようにしたいと思います。

6. 私の同伴の者もこの度逃亡したのは何か悪心あってのことではなく、結局、恥辱でもないことを恥辱と考え、帰国したいとのみ考えて心身が乱れ、御奉行所の御慈悲のご教諭を忘却してのことでございます。そうしたところ、召し捕らえられて、初めてお役所に帰ってきた際、理のない申し訳をいたし、逃亡はロシアの法制にあると申し上げましたところ、御奉行所もただ狼狽した者とお考えいただき、恥じ入るばかりでございます。夷狄には法制度もなく、ワルワルスキ〔訳註：アフリカ地方の国で、ヨーロッパ側が命名したもの。ワルワルとは悪法の意味とのこと〕などという国の法制は笑うべきことのみであります。ヨーロッパ諸国の法制はそれぞれ若干の違いがありますが、誠実を基本としていることは同じ

26

7.

です。逃亡してもよいということがあるなどは、私はこれまで承知していません。結局心身が混乱したためそのように申し立てたのだと思います。御憐察いただきたく存じます。

盗賊や追剥にとらわれた場合や合戦で捕虜になった場合、敵将に対して「義理之詞」を告げなければ逃亡してもよいということはあります。しかしながら私たちはこのようなことまで持参いたしました。全体困窮して国後に来たわけで、日本の御役人の手紙とも実に不思議なことと思います。したがってご援助をお願いしたのであって、それに対して銃丸で御答えになられるとは【訳註：ロシア人は石坂武兵衛の手紙を受け取った上は、日本のどこの地方に行ってもかまわない、かつ願いの義も早速かなうと心得て、着船の翌朝、カピタンが端艇で上陸したところ、日本側から厳しく鉄砲を撃ちかけられて上陸できなかった。手紙の返答に鉄砲の弾を与えたということになりこのように書いてたという】。やむをえず少々の古くなったものなどを頂きましたが、その場合も銅板とわずかばかりの贈り物なども致しました。その後、上陸してこれら頂きました品物の対価を差し上げ、御断り申し上げようと思ったところ、召し捕らえられ、盗賊同様の扱いを受け、まだ吟味が終わっていないけれど、御奉行所にては私どもをお許し下さり、御慈悲の御取り扱いとなってありがたき幸せと存じます。法に照らして吟味中はどのような理由があろうとも逃亡することはできないということは言うまでもないことです【訳註：吟味中はどのような理由があろうとも逃亡はできないと

いうことはヨーロッパの法には明記されていないが、たとえ無罪であっても吟味中は謝罪するべきであって、いわんや有罪の場合でも、どのような言い訳がたつにせよ、罪状が決まらないうちに逃亡するのは、どうなるか分からないのでこのように書いたのであろうという」。このように御慈悲のみて繋がるときは逃亡など考えないものですが、もし御役人のほうで私どもを大盗賊として御仕置きになることになっていても、罪をゆるすこともあるので、士道としては恥すべきことがないよう覚悟はしているものです。古来より高位高官や有徳の士までもが獄舎につながれ、御仕置き場で人生を終わるようなこともあるので、万が一御仕置きとなっても、罪をゆるすかどうかは自分たちには及ぶところでなく、神またはロシア皇帝によって救われるものでありましょう。当春になっても一向に御沙汰がなく、逃亡に不同意の私とアレクセイを欺いて逃亡するなどといったことは、とにかく故郷を思ってのことで、思慮もあいまいなまま行ったことだろう思います。ロシアの諺に「溺れる者は何かに取りつく」というものがあります。たとえ刃物を差し出しても、指が切り落とされようが取りつくものといいます。私同伴の者たちも実にこの諺同様のことにございます。どうかこのことをお察しくださり、御奉行所には広大のご慈悲ご憐憫にてお話し下さり誠にありがたく、私は心中をすべて開陳し、このうえは私自身の恥辱、士道にもとることなく、細かに書き上げ、御奉行所の前に差し上げるべきが当然と考えます。

8.

1806年〔訳註：我が国の文化3年に相当〕春末頃、ロシア官船ナデジタ〔訳註：船名。レザノフ乗船。長崎来航の船〕并アメリカンカンパニー商船ネワ〔船名〕は、世界一周の最初の航海に出発しました。無事の航海で本国でも喜んでいたが、この航海中日本使節だけが遂行することがかなわなかったのです。ナデジタ号の船長クルーゼンシュテルンほか乗船士官たちは、この使節が成功しなかったことを話し合ったが、レザノフが性格が性急で高慢なため、使節の任に堪えざることが数々あったこと、かつ日本の習俗が疑うことが何かと多く、ヨーロッパと異なることがあって、同盟の盟約を交わすことができなかったこと、これが不成功の第一の理由だということになったのです。また、その節だれひとり注意せず、レザノフは通訳をつけなかったので、オランダ人が通訳をしました。これに日本役人やロシア人が心を寄せたものであったとて、この者が姦計をめぐらすなど考えもしませんでしたが、どうやら姦計をめぐらしたようです。私たちの船ジアナ号は、西暦1807年〔訳註：我が国の文化6年に相当〕の冬、イギリスのポーツマスに停泊中にこのことが思いもよらず発覚したのでございます。

このことは知らないことではありますが、レザノフに対する日本側の返答を勘案するに、日本はロシアとは大いに離れているので習俗もかなり違っています。ヨーロッパの習俗も大いに分からないので、日本のためになるかどうかもよく分かりません。私はナデジタ号

の士官バロナビリン〔訳註：我が国の大名・旗本等の称号という。このほかギニヤセ、カラフなどがある。これらは以下にたびたび出てくる。キニヤセ、ガラフ、その次がバロナである。もっともバロナであるが、原文にそうあるので本文のような翻訳をした〕ザヲジン〔姓名〕やそのほかの士官から聞きましたが、長崎において仰せ渡された趣は、再び日本の地に来ることは許されないこと、またもし日本船がロシアに漂着した場合は、ロシア本国役人からオランダに依頼し、オランダから長崎に護送するようにとのことで、これ以降日本のこといったいどのような趣意なのか本国の者たちは分からないとのことでありました。このことは、とはまったく考慮しないようにして、ほかの国々と交易をすると役人や商人たちは考えたのでございます〔訳註：本文にあるアメリカンカンパニーとは、アメリカ地方の産物を取り扱う商人たちの会社である〕。アメリカ地方は国王が開発した場所ではなく、先年商人たちが初めて開拓した場所で、役人は駐在していない。先年オホーツク辺りから商人が銘々思い思いに船を出し、アリューシャン列島からアメリカ地方へ航海して交易し、相互に産物を集めあるいは求めるところから争論に発展し、年々死傷者も少なくなかった。また貪欲な商人が先住民を辱めたりすることも多く、イルクーツクの豪商センボノ〔岩下註：シェリホフなので、「セリホフ」の誤写と思われる〕という者が、年々来航する商人たちを集めて会社を設立した。これにより争論が止み、先住民の撫育にもなるとしたため国王や諸役人も

30

承認し、会社法を授けた。その結果、アメリカンカンパニーと称し、社屋を建設し、大商人が集まり金銀を出資して、アメリカの産物を取り扱うことになった。ネワ号は、同社の持ち船である。会社所属のバラノフが会社設立時からアメリカに航海したが、カジャッカ〔岩下註：コディアック〕という昔からの村がある場所に要害を作り、それからヤコタツ〔岩下註：ヤクタット〕というところに村を建設し、それぞれ家臣を置いて守護させ、それからシイツカ〔岩下註：シトカ〕という島に渡り、ここにも村を作り、このカジャッカとヤコタツの両地を先住民のために一度焼き払い、先住民との争論に発展した。その後再び両島に村を建設し商人が住んでいた。その後、ノーワラハンゲリスコイというところに大要塞を建設し、商人バラノフの住居は役所同様となり、本国船はおよそこの場所に停泊した。

バラノフは当時コメルジーソウエチニという商人の官名をもらっていた。この地方の総官同様の役目であった。しかしながらこの地方は離れた辺境地帯で、とかく不便でボストン〔訳註：別名、イルトアメリカ〕などへ毎年航海して交易をしていた。持参の品の内、鉄砲・鉛玉・焔硝など持ち込み、先住民と交易する地方では、実に暴虐の夷族の場合はこれらの品物を渡さずとも隠しておかなかったので、これらが渡ってしまうと安心できないので、首都ペテルブルクの会社総官のものと申し合わせ、年一艘ずつ、官船をノーワラハンゲリスコイへ派

遣し、ボストン人がやってきてもこれら武器の交易はできないことを願い出た。かつ総官の役人が一人派遣され、これに願い出て、本国役人がボストンへ趣き、これらの始末を相談したところ、同所の役人が言うことには、これらの品物を持ってきた船があれば、船員も逮捕してもよく、国法によって処罰することととなった。アメリカ地方総官の役人一人〔役名〕ボコウニキ〔姓名〕コーハというものがオホーツクから出発し、カムチャッカにて亡くなった。私どもの船もこれらのことでネワ号と同じく出帆を命じられた〕。〔〇本文で日本の考えがわからないとするところは、カムチャッカは日本には近く、これらは自国の船にて送ることは許されず、この地方に漂着した日本人をロシア本国からオランダに依頼して、オランダからバタビヤに回して日本へ送還することは海陸何千里にもなり、寒暖温熱の地方を引き回しせっかく保護した者も多くが途中で病死してしまう状況となる。地球の遠近は当方も分かっており、このような趣は理由もなく、またヨーロッパの変革はオランダから時々伝達されていることと思われるが、年ごとに敵味方が相変わることも多く、ヨーロッパも自由に通行できないこともありえる。これらはわれわれもよく分かっていることだ。このようなわけで、前条のようにいわれると漂流民は送っても送らなくてもどうでもいいというように聞こえる。国を知られ、人民を招き撫育する御徳はすでに夷島にも及んでいるのだから、このようなことはいわれなきこと。今、アレキサンダー皇帝は当方の思

9.

　どのような国も同じであるが、商人は武士や農民とは違うことを行うものであります。

北アメリカの船が、同所のロシア領地の内にて、年々交易を行っていたところ、至って宜しくない品物を持ってきていたので、ロシアから来た者や外海を航海する者はいろいろ支障が出ていました。それで同所の会社の長から、これらの品物を持ってくるものは本国経由で差し止めにするように取り計らってくれるように申し立てました。これらの商人たちの考えには官船一艘ずつ年々ごとにアメリカ領にやってくれれば、たとえボストン人がやってきて悪事をなすことはすまいとのこと、ロシア領アメリカ会社が完成した時から、ネワ号をノーワハンゲリスコイというところへ荷物を送り、その場所にてその地の産物を積み込んで広東へ向かい交易を行い、それから本国に帰るのでございます。これらについて海上総官の役人たちがかねがね考えていることは、官物の輸送もネワ号同様の荷物を積み込んでいるので、これらをオホーツクに回せば宜しいのではないか。会社の申し立てもあって、ジアナ号が出来次第荷物をオホーツクへ輸送し、かつ、我々はネワ号の警備をすることを命じられました。アヅミラリテースキム・テバルターメンタ〔岩下註：海軍省〕とい

惑を分からないとして、交易を願ってもその後お取り上げにならない、結局ヨーロッパは遠隔地なので国情も伝わりにくく、隣接している国なのに協力し合うことも出来ないことは本国もよく知っている〕

う役所にて荷物・食糧そのほか医療器具等に至るまで取りそろえ渡された。その際、ウヲエノイ・テバルターメンタよりゴローウニン艦長〔訳註：これまでガワビンと言ってきたカピタンの名前であるが、言語で聞いたときはガワビンと聞こえたが、文字にするとゴローウニンとするのがよろしく、このように翻訳する〕へ測量器具幷書籍・地図そのほかインストルクチヤ〔岩下註：通達のこと〕という海路指南書の写しを渡されました。その際、〔役名〕ケニヤラウマヨロ〔姓名〕ガマンヤという者から書面で命じられたことは、ゴローウニンが航海するあいだ多くの国々や島々があり、昔から多くの航海者が詳しく測量をしているとはいえ、この度は詳しく調査して漏れがないようにせよ、また、オホーツクやクリル諸島も今なお詳しくなっていないところもあるので、オホーツクに至る海路や時間をみつけてこの地方のことを記述すること、またイギリスでは新版の地球図や海路指南書を買い整えることを命じられました。10月下旬〔訳註：1806年10月下旬、我が国では9月から10月の間〕にはネワ号も荷物を積み込んでいたが、ジアナ号を銅噴きする作業が終わっていなかったため、ネワ号だけで出帆し、ジアナ号は延期していました。その後さまざまな命令がありましたが、1806年冬〔訳註：ロシアでは12月・1月・2月のこと。我が国の11月・12月・1月に当たる。これ以下の冬はこれに相当する〕になり、海上総官の役人〔役名〕モスコイミニースクラ〔姓名〕ハウエウワシレウイチ・チーチャコフ〔岩下註：パヴェル・ヴァシリエヴィチ・

34

チチャゴフという者からジアナ号の造作ができ次第、再びカムチャッカ地方へ荷物を輸送するよう命じられました。

10.

翌1807年【訳註：我が国の文化4年に当たる】7月下旬ジアナ号造作がすべて終了し、士官・水兵等乗組員に国王の命令書が与えられました。それによれば、荷物をカムチャッカに輸送し、アメリカに向かいそこでネワ号と合流し、航海中は警戒を怠らず、広東港に赴き、ネワ号交易が済み次第、ネワ号とともにペテルブルクに帰還すべしとの命令でした。その際、国王はフルシィイヤより帰りカランシタツ要塞や官船数艘見分のついで、国王自身はジアナ号見分をしました。

これらの乗組員の名前は別に下に記しました。

11.

1807年7月25日【訳註：文化4年3月末ころ】ジアナ号はカランシタツを出帆し、ホメラニアというところに到達しました。その際、大砲の音がおびただしく聞こえました。そこで本船はロシアのそれよるデンマークのコペンハーゲンというところに着船し、その手前でイギリス船に出会い、同船から何国の国籍で、行き先はどこかを尋ねられました。そこで、カムチャッカに荷物を送るために派遣された船であることをゴローウニン艦長が答えました。それより段々右都に近寄ったところ、入津し、例の通り旗合わせかたがた案内の船が派遣されてきました。またおびただしい数のイギリス船を見受けました。これらの案内人が申すには「イギリス船がこのように首都を取り囲んでいるのはデンマークの官

船がイギリスに派遣されると聞いてそのようにやっているとのこと。デンマークの役人は不承知であり、合戦の用意をしている」とのことです。その日の夜鉄砲による小競り合いがあったようです。その夜、イギリス軍船がジアナ号の脇を通過したが、城中からおびただしく大砲を打ちかけたため、ついにイギリス船は焼失しました。また焼け残りの船はジアナ号の脇を流れていきました。翌日、同所役人〔役名〕コモンドル〔姓名〕ドヲケン幷この地の総官〔姓名〕ハイナという者と対面したが、両人が言うことには「ただ今ご覧いただいている通り合戦中にて、当所に滞留することはできないので、デンマーク領エリチノルへ行ってもらいたい」とのことでした。そこでコペンハーゲンを早速に出帆しました。

その夜は沖で滞留しましたが、その翌日の朝から合戦が始まりました。その後、エリチノルに到着しましたが、そこで食料少々と水などを補給しました。2日後、イギリスに向けて出帆しました。海上では烈風に襲われ、さらに各国の艦船を多く目撃しました。それよりカレ〔訳註：フランス・イギリスの境にある地峡〕というところに至ってイギリス船に遭遇し、先方からいろいろ尋ねられたので、ゴローウニン艦長がデンマークで答えたのと同じように回答しました。こうしてクロンシュタット出帆より40日程を経て、イギリスの港ポーツマスに着岸しました。ここでうわさを聞いたところ、イギリスは近いうちにロシアと戦争をするつもりらしいとのこと。この港に先だって寄港しているロシア官船シベリア

号のホウリン艦長からも話を聞きました。ところでゴローウニンはイギリスの首都ロンド
ンへ行き、船中の必需品を買い整えました。また本国からの指令通り広東または喜望峰に
てもブラジリアにも金銭受け取りの為替手形等、商人と相談しもらい受けました。その節、
ロンドン詰のロシア役人バラン・アラベウスという者に出会い、イギリスとロシアが戦争
となればジアナ号の航海も困難になるのでどうしたらいいだろうと相談しました。する
と自分は海上のことは不案内であり、本地にかかわらないこともできない
ので、返答は難しいということになりました。ロンドン詰ロシア役人〔役名〕ボロウニヤ〔姓
名〕ケレイカという者にも相談しました。同人が言うには、「地方巡境船」〔下札：本文に
ある巡境船と言うのはイギリスで出版された新聞の中にそのように記してある。そこで別
冊抜書を翻訳して差上げた〕であることを言い、当所にて添え状を貰うことができれば、
途中難儀もないだろうとのことでした。それでイギリス役人〔姓名〕セキリタリヤ〔役名〕
カニシカと言う者から添え状を貰うことができました。〔訳註：本文にロシアの役人がロン
ドンに詰めている件であるが、ヨーロッパの法では同盟の国には役人1名か2名ずつ相互に配置
することになっている。ただし「地方巡境船」は敵船に出会っても奪い取られることがない。こ
れはヨーロッパの慣習法なのである〕

　ゴローウニン艦長がロンドンに滞在中に、副艦長リコルドはイギリスのヒリワウムアゲ

ントムという役職のブロウノムという人物と接触しました。同人が言うことには、先ごろオランダ船がバタビアよりオランダに帰国する途中でイギリス船がこれを拿捕しました。

それで我々がその船を受け取りましたが、船中の書物のうちに、長崎関係書状が２通あり、一通は長崎在留オランダ出役のものからオランダ国〔役名〕コロス・ベンシオネル〔姓名〕シンメリベリニングという者への書状、もう一通はクルーゼンシュテルン〔訳註：レザノフが長崎に来航した際の艦長である〕への書状でした。第一のシンメリベリニングへの書状にはロシア使節レザノフが長崎に来航した時に通訳を伴わなかったのでわれらオランダ人が通訳をしたが、ロシアの願いが聞き届けられないように取り計い、なるべく使節を悪く取り計らったため、当初の目的通りになった。このように取り計らったので、我々の日蘭貿易には有益なようになったので報告するというものでした。第二のクルゼンシュテルンへの書状には、よく分からなかったが、クルーゼンシュテルンへの親愛の情を著した手紙のようでした。ブロウノムはこれらの書状を持参し、通訳してリコルドに聞かせた。

リコルドはこの件を本国に報告すべく書面をしたためました。ブロウノムも添え状を認め追って差し出してほしいと依頼したところ、承知して、同人が言うことには、ただこのことが諸方面で風評になった場合、大切な使節が通訳も連れず、オランダに謀られたということになってはロシアの恥辱となり、これだけが気の毒だと話したと言います。

ゴローウニン艦長はブロウノムの添え状と広東丼喜望峰〔訳註：先年オランダ領になった

もの。オランダがフランスに併合された時、フランス領になったが、近年イギリスがここを奪い、

現在イギリス領になっている〕等の為替手形を受け取り、必要な諸品を買い整え、ポーツマ

スに帰ってきました。その際、イギリス船がデンマークの船をコペンハーゲンから拿捕し

てきたことを見ました。それからさらに食糧や薪・水など買い取り、ブラジリアに向け出

帆した。イギリス滞在は２カ月ばかりにおよびました。ここからブラジリアまでの海上で

は厳しい雨風に見舞われました。それで艀船壱艘を失い、帆柱を破損しました。海上では

マテクエという島やイギリス・ハルトウリア・アメリカ等の船を見かけました。70日でブ

ラジリアの港エカラリネに入津し、ここで食糧薪水を調達し、破損した帆柱を取り替えて、

正月中旬にゴルミ岬〔訳註：南アメリカの岬名〕に赴き、岬近くに来たところで烈風激し

く気候もよくなく、船中病人が多く発生し、その上、船上で漏水も多くなり、やむを得ず

アフリカ喜望峰に帰還しました。この海上でテリスラシダリシカという島を見て、さらに

烈風にたびたび遭遇しました。それから喜望峰の港シモンスクへ入港しました。イギリス

のキャプテン〔姓名〕コレーベツ〔訳註：ゴローウニンがよく知っているものである〕丼レイ

チャナンド〔役名〕〔名前不詳〕が、ジアナ号にやってきました。ゴローウニン艦長は「我々

はコルミ岬に到達したが、烈風に難儀してここにやってきました。食料を調達し、船の破

損を修繕し、病人を養生させてほしい」と依頼しました。コレーベッツは直ちに自船に戻り、武装した兵士を引き連れ言うことには、「近々イギリスとロシアが戦争になるので、このジアナ号も拿捕することになる」とのことでした。ゴローウニン艦長はイギリス役人の添え状を見せ、本船は「地球巡境船」であることを言って聞かせました。するとレイチャンド〔役名〕〔名前不詳〕は添え状を受け取り、ジアナ号に2人ほどを残して、本船に帰っていきました。この間、機密書類をイギリス側に没収されることを恐れ、ゴローウニン艦長はそれらを隠したり焼き捨てたりしました。その後カブシタツ〔訳註：シモンスグ最寄りの港で、イギリス役人が常駐〕の役人〔役名〕コモンドル〔姓名〕ロレいう者が、〔役名〕ヒリゾウエム〔訳註：敵船を拿捕する役職〕を連れて、シモンスクにやって来ました。彼らが言うことには「ロシアの役人からどのような命令を受けたのか聞きたい」とのこと。そこでウチェノイテバルタメンタよりの書付を差し出し、見させたところ、「先のレイチャナンドに渡した添え状も不備があり、役人の書付も専ら地理見分ということも出来ないので、イギリス本国に問い合わせたうえで出帆許可をする。それまではこの港で待機せよ。」となってしまいました。そしてイギリス士官〔名前〕ムーデという者がジアナ号に来て警備することになりました。

およそ5か月ほどたてば本国から沙汰もあろう」とのこと。それまではこの港で待機せよ。

その後、イギリス本国から多くの船がやってきました。その他、〔役名〕アヅミラウ〔名

前）バルチなどという者も到着しました。およそ6か月もたちましたが、何の沙汰もなく、ゴローウニン艦長はカブシタツに赴き、以前イギリスで商人より受け取った為替手形で金銭に換金したついでに、バルチや商人から聞いたところでは、「イギリス本国からの返答はすでに来ているようです。それによればジアナ号からの申し出は疑わしいところはあるけれど、本国の添え状も遣わしたことであるし、それをイギリスの役人が指揮して奪い取ることも出来かねるとのことです。それゆえいつまで待っても出帆許可は急には出ないでしょう」とのことでした。そこでゴローウニン艦長は熟考して「イギリス・ロシアの戦争はいつ終わるか分からない。そのままここに逗留しても炎熱地方故荷物も破損してしまうだけだ。船もだんだん痛んでいるし、乗員の給与も遠隔地故格別多く支給しなければならないこともある」と考えました。そこで海上上役の者に逃亡を相談したのです。ところで港が2か所あるところの慣習では、年々港を替えて滞留することになっていました［訳註：5月より10月はシモンスク港、11月より4月まではストロフェ港、これらは風によるとのこと］。それでこの節、追々外港に赴くことになり、また番船も出港するなど、ジアナ号警固のイギリス士官ムーデもそれらの番船に乗り組むことを命じられ出帆しました。これはチャンスと水や薪を調達し、また目立たないようになるべく多くの食料を買い入れ仕度をしました。するとイギリス役人〔官名〕アヅミラウ〔姓名〕バルチはこの様子を見て、キャプテン・

トムキンソスに「ゴローウニン艦長は命令がなければ出帆を許されない。証拠の書面はそのまま保全せよ」と命じ、ジアナ号に派遣し、その旨を伝達しました。やむを得ずゴローウニン艦長は士官の連名で「我々は逃亡はヨーロッパにおいて大いに恥ずべきことと知っています」という書面を提出しました。しかしながら、その後、次第に物価が上昇し、手持ちの金も日々目減りして、新鮮な食料も調達できず、イギリス人からも渡されず、かつ荷物の破損も著しく、そこでゴローウニン艦長は逃亡を企画しました。外で航海していた船も港に戻ってきて港内に多くの船が滞留するようになったので、ゴローウニン艦長は、アヅミラルに手紙を認め1809年5月中旬ころ〔訳註：我が国の文化6年4月ころ〕順風をまって、出港しました。海上では大船〔訳註：どこの船かは分からない〕一艘を遠望しました。

たびたび烈風に出会い難儀し、タナ島〔訳註：東西経度約165、6度、赤道約16、7度、小島でどこの国にも属していない。先住民のみ居住する島で、特に熱帯地帯である〕に立ち寄り、食糧・水・薪などを調達し、9月下旬カムチャッカに到達しました。

ジアナ号が喜望峰にいた時分、イギリス軍艦が一艘立ち寄りました。これはカムチャッカ地方からアメリカのロシア領に建設された村を略奪するためにイギリス本国から派遣されたものでありました。カムチャツカ到着後ゴローウニン艦長はブラジリア以来喜望峰の次第幷イギリス軍艦の件を詳しく認めロシア本国海上上役に送りました。喜望峰での顛末

は好ましくない事案であり、すべての国王の怒りを買うことであるが、ロシア国王は憐憫の者が多く、願いの筋はたいてい聞き届けてくれるのであります。

ペトロパブロフスキーの役人のキャプテン・モーチャノフとニツネがカムチャッカより赴任して来ました。〔役名〕ホッボコウニキ〔姓名〕シベリヤコフという者など、当時この地方の役人〔役名〕ゲネラウマヨロ〔姓名〕コセレフと〔役名〕マヨロ〔姓名〕モナコフ、同クルブスコイは、ペトロパブロフスキーの先の役人でありましたが、退役したことを聞きました。その際、当時の役人〔役名〕ゲネラウマヨロ〔姓名〕ベトロスコイ幷ロシア領アメリカ会社の総支配人ハレフニコフが言ったことには、「フヴォストフとダヴィドフが、日本の村落において乱暴を働いたことから、オホーツクにおいて二人を逮捕し入獄を命じた。彼らの同船者は役人が検分して、荷物はすべて封印の上、倉に置いている。このフヴォストフとダヴィドフはいったん牢獄から逃亡した。しかし、再び逮捕され、ペテルブルクに送られたので、吟味のうえ刑罰に処せられると思われるが、同人らの親類には高貴の者もいるので助命嘆願などもあり、贖罪のためスウェーデンとの戦争に派遣された。彼らはどこでも見事な働きをしたので、免罪にはなっていないが、上記のシベリアコフ幷モウチャラの側近として勤務している。同人が言うことには相違がない」とのことです。なお、現在船船を厳しく検査していることは皆、フヴォストフ一件に起因しているとのことです。

その後、私が聞いたところでは、レザノフは日本の御役人方よりのお返事が心にひっかかり、フヴォストフに命じて、会社の船で日本に赴き、乱暴を働くよう口上で依頼したとのことです。そうしたところ、この命令のことをクルーゼンシュテルン艦長が知って、フヴォストフを呼んで「貴殿がレザノフの命令を実行したら、厳しく処罰されるので思い止まるように」と申し諭したが、フヴォストフはいったん承諾したとのこと。そうしたところ、レザノフは日本に持ち渡ろうとした荷物を会社の船〔船号〕マリヤという船に積み込んで、自分も乗り組み、フヴォストフとダヴィドフを同行させて、ノーワアラバンゲリスコイ〔訳註：北アメリカロシア領の地名〕に赴きました。そこで越冬し、ボストン船〔船号〕ユノナという船を買い受け、上記の荷物を積みいれ、またフヴォストフとダヴィドフを同行させてカリフォルニア〔訳註：アメリカの内ロシア領の南に所在〕へ赴き、そこで荷物をすべて売り払いカムチャッカに戻ってきたのです。この際、レザノフはたいへん重要なことを思いついて、考えを変えたのです。すでにオホーツクに出立する際に、文書をもってフヴォストフに命じたことは、先に命じた日本行きに関しては必ず中止せよ、そのほか不心得のことはしてはならぬと申し渡したところ、フヴォストフは承諾したと返答しましたが、その後、盟友に話したところ、「惜しむようなものでもないロシアの菽で囲った羊はそれを食べたとしても許してやるべきだ」といった〔訳註：これはロシアの諺で、羊がロシア菽を

好んで食べることを知っていながら囲いを開けておき、羊がロシア菘を食べつくしたあとにやってきて、菘を惜しんでも間に合わないという意味である。フヴォストフが戦闘好きということはレザノフはかねがね知っていた、船まで与えておいて今更中止の命令を出しても間に合わないということを意味している）

それでフヴォストフが最初の乱暴を始めて、カムチャッカに帰ってきて、どのような偽りを申し立てたのか、役人たちも知らなかったのですが、冬の末になって〔役名〕ゲネラウマヨロ〔姓名〕コセレフは、初めてフヴォストフの事実を認識し、逮捕すべしと考えました。これらはフヴォストフの朋友より報せがあったため、早春で海にはまだ氷があったが、フヴォストフはそれを砕いて逃亡したとのこと。それで逮捕ができなかったので、〔役名〕ゲネラウマヨロ〔姓名〕コセレフ幷ペトロパブロフスキーの役人マヨロ〔姓名〕モナコフ、ロブスコイの3人は役目をはく奪されました。そうしたところフヴォストフとダヴィドフの2人は続けて日本に対して第二の乱暴事件を起こし、オホーツクに立ち寄り、アメリカに持っていってよい物を調べ、自分たちの罪状を押し隠していましたが、彼らの船中の荷物を扱うニシヤシニコフという者が酒に酔って乱暴の始末をその地のものにすべて話したため、同地の役人〔官名〕ボコウニキ〔姓名〕ブハリンという者が、初めて事実を知り、フヴォストフとダヴィドフを呼び寄せ、乱暴の証拠を探り出し、両人を逮捕し監獄に入れ、船中

45　ムールによる獄中からの上申書　上下

の荷物をすべて封印して没収したとのことです。その船中にいた日本人2人は自由の身となり、厚く保護することを命じられました。しかしながらオホーツク地方は、湿地の上気候も宜しくないので、日本から奪った諸品も倉に入れたままでは、早晩破損してしまうので、ブハリンが交代して跡役のババエフという者がこの地に赴任してきて、フヴォストフの荷物は王都から命令があるはずだが何の沙汰もない。しかし、このように倉に積んでおいても全部腐敗してしまうので、日本に返還するのにとても役立たないことになる、その上、会社は再三損金を出しており迷惑である。万が一返還の場合は金銭であるいは現物で返納するので、どうかこの品物を売り払うことを許してもらいたい、またこの件をイルクーツクの役人に伝達してもらいたいとのことでありました【訳註：本文にオホーツクでフヴォストフが逮捕された時、シヤシニコフが話したところではこの地の役人が承知したところでは、直ちにフヴォストフとダヴィドフを呼び寄せ、どこに行くのか尋問したところ、日本に行って少額の貿易をなさんという偽りを言ったので、そのまま拘束し、下僚の役人に船を捜索させたところ、日本人が2人いるとの話で早速事実が露見したとのことである。○本文にある通り、ババエフが会社縁故があるというのは、同人の妻が会社の商人の娘であるとのこと。○本文にあるように、会社が再三損金を出しているというのは、フヴォストフとダヴィドフが会社に雇われていたため、今回の

46

一件を会社が引き受け取り扱うことになったということである。かつその船の中の物は日本から奪ったものばかりではなく、会社の荷物も積みこんでいたので、没収の際、一緒に封印したため、すべてが会社の損失になってしまったということ」

そうしたところ、2人の日本人もオホーツク滞留がいつ終わるのか分からないまま帰国のことだけを案じていましたが、やむをえず夜分に川船一艘を盗み取り、逃れ去り行方知れずとなっています。このほかカムチャッカ地方でも何人か不明だが、十分に調査していないが、クリル諸島を伝って同様に逃亡した日本人がいるとのことです。しかしながらクリル諸島の者どもはそのような者は見かけていないと言っており、カムチャッカの者たちは海中に沈んでしまったのではないかと言うことです。

不幸なレザノフ〔訳註：これはレザノフが長崎に来航して交易願いを出したにもかかわらず失敗し、帰国の上、不首尾におわったこと、心痛のあまり亡くなったことから、不幸なレザノフと書いたとであるとのことである〕は、帰国途上より、知罪の状を認めた書簡を本国役人に送って訴えました。「どうかお許し願いたい」と数度送ったが、恥辱のあまり痛恨して、ついにカラスノヤルスカというところで死去しました。レザノフの親類ガラワチョフというところで死去しました。レザノフの親類ガラワチョフという者も家柄もよく、特に怜悧なものであったので、レザノフが船中の間、ルイテナントを勤めさせていました。ナデジダ号が帰帆した時、レザノフは致し方が不届きだったことを

恥じ入って、サンテレナ島で自身のこれまでのことを書き留めてから、小銃で自殺したとも言われている〔訳註：本文でレザノフが死んだことに関しては、一説には毒薬を服用して死んだとも言われているが、これらのことはとりとめもない噂話であり、確実なことは言い難いが、毒薬はオピコンといって自殺を覚悟しているものが用いるものという。この毒薬を服用すると起きることができず、命を失くすという〕。

〔下げ札：本文、ガラワチョフが死んだことに関しては、艦長の手控え人名の内に書かれていて、別冊に翻訳し差し上げている〕

以上申し上げた、フヴォストフとダヴィドフはスウェーデン戦争に大功を顕したが、免罪の申し渡しはなかったので、両人ともに酒に溺れ、ついにネワ川に沈んで難儀な一生を終えました。また、ジアナ号の積荷はカムチャッカに置いていた分はすべて陸揚げしました。かつボストン人に関してはアメリカに来ることを命じられたこともあり、かつイギリス軍艦がアメリカ地方に来航することも聞いていたので、やむを得ず春になり、アメリカに赴きました。ゴローウニンはアメリカのやり方が宜しくないとして自身も分かっていましたが、失敗を糊塗する考えで、役人たちにこれまでの経緯を申し聞かせました。なお、ジアナ号はクリル諸島の測量の使命もあったことです。そうしたところゴローウニンが考えたことには、ジアナ号船中の者どもは久しぶりの遠隔地航海で、国家のこと

48

18.

だけを楽しんでいればいいのであって、海上測量に手間取っていることは好まないが、これらの願いをすべて押し隠し、船中の者どもに何も知らせないことになりました。私は船中カピタン・リコルド丼他の者から聞いていました。ゴローウニンが隠していたことは、私が申し上げたことはいかがでしょうか？　何もそうまでして恥すべきことはないのです。

1810年春、ジアナ号はノーワアラハンゲリスコイへ赴き、停泊中に北アメリカの船やボストン船が来航しましたので、それらの船の者から聞きましたところでは、イギリス軍艦が広東からロシア領アメリカに来るとのこと。海上でサンデウイチ島〔岩下註：ハワイ諸島のこと〕〔訳註：本文のサンデウイチという島は、赤道北緯20度ばかりのところにあって、温暖で産物が多く、人物は旧ヨーロッパから来た者と言われているが、当時はこの島で生まれたものが多く、この島の総官の酋長もいて、庶民を撫育している。ヨーロッパの諸船がこの島に立ち寄ると、船員の中にはこの島に留まって帰国しないものなどいるとのことを聞いている〕という島に立ち寄ったところ、多くの者が逃亡し、または病人もいたので、再び広東に帰ったとのことでした。しかしながらこの軍艦は広東で人数を揃え、明年、アメリカ丼カムチャツカへ赴く予定とのことを聞きました。この年9月、ジアナ号はカムチャツカに帰りました。

19

同年春会社のネワ号がアメリカより帰ってきました。この船の中にレイテナント【訳註：

商船にもこの役職はあって、気象観測を任務とする】カゲンメイシテルと言う者より聞いた

ことを書いておきます。このネワ号は1806年10月下旬【訳註：ジアナ号が本国を出帆し

た前年】カランシタツにて食糧・水・薪を積み込み出帆しました。ブラジリアのサンサウ

ワドル【岩下註：ブラジル、サンサルバドル】、ノーハゴランデ【訳註：新オランダ】【岩下註：

現在のオーストラリア】のホルトシヤキリシ【訳註：同所港名】などという所に立ち寄り、

1807年夏ノーワアラハンゲリコスイで帰港し、同所総官バラノフに本国の産物を渡し、

そこで越冬し、1808年広東交易の諸品を同人から受け取ったところ、オホーツクから

の連絡では、ロシア本国とイギリスとが戦争を始めたということで、広東行きを中止しま

した。それからサンデウイチ島に行き、そこの産物や塩そのほかの諸商品を交易して越冬

し、1809年の春、これらの商品をカムチャッカに持ち帰り、そこで荷物替えをして、ノー

ワアラハンゲリスコイへ帰港し、またカムチャッカに荷物積み入れたけれども、この時は

秋で風が良くなく、予定を変え、カシヤカという島【訳註：アリウツケ【岩下註：アリュー

シャン】諸島の中にあるとのこと】に行き、越冬しました。そして1810年カムチャッカ

に帰港しました。このネワ号が1807年初めてノーワアラハンゲリスコイへ来航した時、

その場所で船中荷物取扱の者はトロボギリチコイという者で、今回もネワ号に乗船してい

ましたが、私が出会った時は、ことのほか性格がよく面白い人物でした。同人からの話で
は、契丹・中国・日本その外、サンデウイチ島などに赴いたことなど人づてに聞きました
が、そのことを詳しくお聞きしたいと言いましたら、その人が言うには、以下の通りでした。

トロボギリチコイは北アメリカ〔訳註：ボストン〕船長ヲゲインという者がその場所の荷
物を積み込み広東に行ったところ、トロボギリチコイは全く言語が通じなかったため、交
易事務をヲゲインが専門に取り扱い帰船し、ハラノフ幷トロボギリチコイを偽ったとのこ
とです。その後、またまたヲゲインは広東へ交易したいので諸品を渡してくれるようにバ
ラノフに依頼したところ、今度はバラノフが承知しなかったとのことです。このころレザ
ノフが使節として日本にやってきましたが、願い筋はかなわず、日本は交易はしないとの
趣旨を承りました。ヲゲインは荷物を受け取れるように偽計をめぐらし、バラノフに言っ
たことには、「現在、ロシア船は日本に寄港することはできないが、北アメリカ船は長崎
に寄港することもあるという。荷物を渡してくれれば間違いなく日本に行き、交易して帰っ
てくる」とのこと。バラノフは何事にも不案内なので、ヲゲインの言う所を真実と考え、
荷物を渡し、荷物取扱者1人〔訳註：則ちこのトロボギリチコイである〕、日本役人への書
簡など長崎に持ち込み、停泊しました。その際、どのようなことで来日したのかなどお尋
ねがありましたが、このヲゲインは真実を申し上げると直答し、アメリカ船がヨーロッパ

に寄港した場合、蓄えていた船中の食料があっても乏しくなってくれば、海上では心もと

なく、どうか食料を供給していただきたく、対価としてはアメリカ産の産物を差

し上げることで相殺したくと申し上げました。ただし、日本の役所よりは、「食料は遣わしてもよ

いが、それらの産物は受け取れない。」とのことでした。それよりヲゲインは広東へ行き

交易をして、またまた値段についてはトロボギリチコイを偽ったとのこと。それからヲゲ

インは帰航の際、カムチャツカに立ち寄り、荷物の半分を同所に降ろし、残り半分をアメ

リカに帰港して後、ハラノフは初めてまたヲゲインに騙されたことを知ったが、致し方な

く、それからヲゲインはノーワアラハンゲリスコイから帰ってきたが、破船して、長くノー

ワアラハンゲリスコイに逗留していました。しかし、商売の術もなく、何度もバラノフに

願い出て会社の社員になりました。バラノフは気の毒に思いヲゲインに新船一艘を渡しま

した。ヲゲインはカジャッカという島へ行く途中の海上で、大水のため破船しました。船

員たちは泳いで海岸に上陸し助かりました。ヲゲインとその妻は船を捨てることとし上陸

しましたが、その夜海上に灯りを見ましたがほどなく灯りも見えなくなり、翌朝、ヲゲイ

ンは船がどこに行ったのか分からないという状態でした。トロボギリチコイはこのネワ号

が初めてノーワアラハンゲリスコイへ行ったとき乗り組みを命じられ、その後、サンデウ

イチ島に来たと話したのです。

当年の冬月、ペテルブルクから書状が到来しましたが、一向に命令はなかったのでした。

しかし、オホーツク役人ボツボコウニキ〔姓名〕ミニチキイという者が書状をもたらしたところでは、ジアナ号をオホーツクに赴かせ、何事もペテルブルクへ報告するようにとのことでした。そうしたところ1811年初春、本国役人より命令書が届きました。艦長は

アメリカに赴くこと、しかるべく準備することなど命じられました。この書で、海上役人〔姓名〕デソルウエルセという者から艦長へ命じられたことは艦長から測量の件が上申されたが、この件をその役人が国王に申し上げたところ聴き済となり、すなわちその命令には、

ヲボトツカ地方53度以上の地方よりサンタラツケ〔訳註・島の名前〕また南クリルツケ諸島を測量せよとのことでした。もっとも命令書幷図面は追って差し遣わすとのことでした。

その節、ヲボーツカ役人よりも添え状があり測量はすぐには終わらないので食糧等差支えたならば、ヲポーツカに帰港しそこで調達し渡すことになる。もっとも雑用金幷諸手当金はカムチャツカ役人ペトロスコイより受け取るようにとのことでした。すなわち私の二子はカムチャツカにやってきてここで初めて見ました。それは以下の通りでございます。

冬末の頃〔訳註・我が国正月ごろ〕カムチヤタル〔訳註・この地方に住んでいる異人の総称〕〔岩下註・カムチャッカ半島の先住民イテリメンのこと〕が狩猟に出たところ、今まで見たことがない人を目撃しました。近くの村に連れ帰り、聞いたところ日本人でございまし

た。このカムチヤタル達が集まって介抱して役所に申し出たところ、ゲネラウ士達に命じ
て部隊何人かで、橇（そり）を持たせて派遣しました。

り、役所のあるところに連れ帰り治療させました。日本人は4人いて皆病んでいるところがあ
は、日本から松前に至る海上で難船となり、舵や檣を失い、冬に海上を漂流し遂にカムチャ
ツカ地方に難破船として漂着しました。その際、何人かは溺死しました。上陸した者もど
この村落か分からなかったので北の方に移動しました。大いに寒気に苦しめられ、飢えて
疲労し、何人かは死亡しました。生き残った4人は南に戻って初めてカムチヤタルに出会
い、村落に連れてこられたとのことです。難破船の荷物に関して聞いたところ、酒を積ん
でいたとのことで、その話が本当かどうか確かめるためゲネラウはほかの士達を連れて、
死人の居る場所や難破船の場所を訪ねさせようとして、遠く北方の石多き湾岸を巡回させ
たところ、二つの岩石があるストワベという名の入り江で、船具の折れはしや衣類、莫蓙（ござ）
や筵（むしろ）などが発見されましたが、破損［岩下註：破損した船体］はことごとく深い雪に埋も
れ、見ることができず、それからさらに北の方に行ったところ、死体を発見しました。そ
こでその場所に埋葬し、帰ってくる道すがら新しい山の崩落したところがありました。そ
こで日本の筵を拾いましたので、海岸の崩れた洞穴を捜索しようということで、崩れた岩
など道々取り除いたところ、洞穴の中に九死に一生を得た日本人3人がいるところを発見

しました。すぐに保護して橇に乗せ、港のある村落に連れてきましたが、非常に飢えており、傷ついているところも多く、役所のあるところまでは連れてくることができないでいます。私は、これら4人の者をたびたび見ることがありました。この場所にて大和尚〔岩

下註：ロシア正教の聖職者か〕ヒヲラという者の家に「第一之座敷」があり、食べ物もみな和尚と同様に出しています。皆が話しをしているところでは、僧1人、外商人1人、3人目は小船頭、4人目は船子で、そのほかの3人は皆船子とのこと。これらの者が持ってきた仏像は、ローシヤと神主が1か所に置死した者がいたとのこと。これらの者が持ってきた仏像は、ローシヤと神主が1か所に置かれ、そのほか介抱のことは日本人の望みに任せ、自国の者と同様に取り扱っています。

異国に漂着した場合は、彼らは安心はできないかもしれないが、彼等が不自由なことはないと思います。御奉行所においても御心配はなされずともよろしいかと存じます。

私はこれらの金銭を受け取りにペトロハウスコイに帰港しました時は4月下旬でジアナ号も用意ができましたので、その翌日出帆しました。ゴローウニン艦長が考えたところでは、オホーツク港は夏でなくては入港することが難しい場所であるので、これを待っていたのでは春中むなしく日を送ることになる。したがってオホーツクに赴くことは好ましくない、クリル諸島の中にも港があるから、また少々食料や薪・水を入手することもあろうから、クリル諸島からザンダルツケへ渡航し、オホーツク地方も巡境のみで、測量は一度

で終わらせ、本国へ帰国することにしよう、本国の命令を考えるとイギリス軍とは遠からず和睦すると思われるので、船中に蓄えた食料も倹約して、約3か月ばかりの食料もあるので、オホーツクに向かって手間取ることはよろしくないとして、まずは南下したのでした。【訳註：9月中、我が国は4月ごろ】烈風に逢い、船中に水が入り食料が多く腐敗してしまいました。思いがけず船中にネズミも多く、食料を多く食い尽くしてしまいました。それより初めてラダワケ、ケトイなどの諸島を見かけ、ラクワケとフショウ島の間へ行こうと考えたが、潮路が強くかつ逆風でずいぶん吹き戻され、それからケトイに接近したので、私は上陸しましたが、住民はいませんでした。この島を回ったところシモシリを見かけました。それからウセシリに行き、船中ヲルダコウは上陸したがその次第は、すでにボカザニエ【訳註：去る冬差上げた上申書】に詳しく書いた通りでございます。

この人物はこの島にて銅製の薬缶并木綿の小切れなど見かけたので、先住民にどこから入手したものか尋ねたところ、先住民が答えていうには、冬末ごろシモシリにて難破船があったがそこから取ったものだと言いました。そこでその船はどこからの船で、乗り組み人数など尋ねましたが、人数はすべて海に没し、船はどこの船かは分からないが、ロシア船ではないとのことでありました。そうしたところ薬缶や木綿などは、ヲルタコフが考え

たところでは、イギリス船ではないかとゴローウニン艦長が言ったというので、そこから
ラショワ島を回ってヤコーシケンに上陸し、そこに住んでいた先住民に申し聴かせたとこ
ろでは、これらウセシリ人の言うことは事実であろうと、かつ、この島の先住民の大人数
はシモシリ、ウルップに住居していることを話しました。それから艀船をシモシリに派遣
し、港の水深を測量しましたが、霧が濃くて着岸が困難でありました。それから艀船をヲーセ
失い、且潮に流され方角を失い、チリボイ島を回り霧の中から海岸を見て、濃霧で度々島を見
査をしましたが、ウルップ島と認めてあったのでまた船を回して、シモシリの港をヲーセ
口というところへハレブニコフを派遣し、水深を計ったところ、港口は至って浅く、ジア
ナ号は入津できなかったのです。それからヤコーシケンは艀船でやって来て、野菜を取り
ましたが、この度は先住民がいなかったのですが、竪穴の住居跡は存在しました。その中
に船の帆が積んであるのが見受けられました。この帆はヨーロッパのものではありません
でした。それからウルップに行き、港を訪ねようと思っていたところ、濃霧にて島々を見
分けることができず、わずかに山や海の岸が見える程度でしたので、何島とも分からない
状態でした。霧が少し落ちて、見える時期がありましたが、ジアナ号はすでに島周辺にい
たのですが、何島とも分からない状態でした。

の度書面を認めた通りに翻訳したところ、ハレブニコウということであったので、本文の通りに直した〕

〔下札：本文シモリシ難破船の趣は船がよほどの大船にて全体赤色に塗られ、ウセシモリ、先住民が申すには帆の布の切れ端はムールが直ちに見たところ、当地にて下し置かれたものの外、縫い足袋の裏によく似た布であった。かつまた最初に下された薬缶の形は、イギリス製の形と少しも違いがなく、ムールは日本船にも同様のものがあるものなのか、考え合わせるところもあって詳しく認めたのである〕

ウルップなのか、海図で確認しましたところ、ウルップとエトロフの両島の間に島があるように認めてあったのです。かつ、南の方に高い山も見え、霧が晴れるに従い、高山の手前の島は分かれているようにも見えていましたので、皆で考えて、遠方に見える島はエトロフ島で、近い島に小船や草で作った小屋や畑などが見えていたので、ゴローウニンはこの島の名前と港に関しては、食物などのことを聞いてくるように私に命じたのでございます。艀船にて上陸し、初めて日本に所属する島の由承りました。その後、クリル人や日本人に聞いたところではこの島はエトロフでありました。とても驚きました。これから私たちが日本の御役人に対応したことは先だって提出しました上申書に書いてございます通りですので文は省略いたします。初めてクナシリに渡航し、ゴローウニンが上陸した時は、

58

エトロフ御役人の御手紙があり、全く異心をさしはさむようなことはなく、クナシリ御役人の御取り扱いはいかにも私分を申しておりません。その後は兵器を携えて来たけれど、浮き桶を差し出した後、その桶の中にあった絵図面を拝見したところ、かつ先住民がゴローウニンに話した趣旨にて思し召しのほどがよく分かったのでございます。その後、上陸した時は、実に本国に上陸したような気持ちになって全く別心なく、その後、クナシリ御役人が食物を下さることをお話しになられた時、人数の多少により下し置かれることをお聞かせいただきましたので、ゴローウニンは余計にいただくつもりで人数を増やし、お答え申し上げた次第でございます。その節、御役人がレザノフが長崎に来航して、日本から渡された趣を承知しているかどうかお尋ねになられましたが、言語も分からず、万が一聞き違いもあった場合、お疑いを受けてはまずいと思い、レザノフは長崎に来航したことは知っているけれども、どのようなことを仰せ渡されたのか、その後もよく分からないとお答えいたしました。

　私たちが日本に来たときは、御免許をいただいたわけではございませんが、イギリス人も免許をいただいたわけではなく、同国人ブロートン〔岩下註：1796年蝦夷地絵鞆―現、室蘭市に来航。蝦夷地沿岸部を測量した。「噴火湾」の命名者。〕という者も先年松前に来航した時、懇篤な応接をいただいたことを同人から聞きました。そのうえ、ブロートン来航の

始末は、同人が残すところなく記載して刊行した書物があり、それなどを見ると、私たちが択捉に来航した際、日本の御役人がお取り扱いになったやり方が、この書物に書かれているところと符合しました。それで国後に来航した時は誠に喜び合っておりました。ところが、御役人の格別に違ったお取り扱いに出会い、やむを得ず一旦はわがままに食物など頂戴しましたが、その後、絵図面によるご問答もありましたので安心しましたが、一向に網に追い込まれたことも気づかず、終に逮捕され厳しい取り扱いを受けることになり、なんとも難儀なことになりました。その後、牢に入れられ、追々フヴォストフの虚偽の書面やクリル人の上申書などの件でご吟味を蒙り、ここに至っては全く帰国の願いもかなわないと力を落とし、覚悟もしましたが、ともかくもロシアが恋しく、士道や才智もともに蒙昧となり、逃亡しようと言いだしましたが、だんだんそれも立ち消えになりました。当冬末【訳註：我が国の正月のころのこと】になり、またまた逃亡したいと思うようになり、その節、彼らが相談しているときに密かに聞いたところでは、重大な難点のあるアレクセイを置いていくことになり、私はこのアレクセイからよろしくない取り扱いを受けていましたので、そうなるとどのような目にあうか分からないため恐ろしくなりました。しかも私は同伴の者たちを売ったとは思わず、いろいろ考えをめぐらしました。これまで私は艦長の意向に逆らってきたので、艦長は私一人を外すような取り扱いをしましたので、この度

は私からこの逃亡の件を日本側に漏らすことは当然であり、かつ艦長は不安だったので、昔のことを思い出させ、何事も昔の儘と言い含め、私から問い合わせても彼らの心中は詳しく分からなかったのです。かつアレクセイにもこのことを知らせ、理解させて、私とアレクセイが互いに悪心を抱くようにさせ、このように恥辱をしのび、偽りをめぐらしたことでございます。〔訳註：同伴の者を売ったことに関して、このことを日本人に知らせた場合、ムール一人が善人で、他の者は悪人となるので、「売った」という表現を忌にしたとのこと。艦長が昔のことを思い出させたというのは、船中では総司令官は自分で、命令の通り誰一人違反するものはなかったのに、ムールがだんだん艦長の言うことを拒絶するようになったことを艦長が述懐したとのことである〕

以上の次第ですので、私から逃亡のことを聞いたところ、艦長は大いに喜んだのでございます。その際、アレクセイはどうするのか聞きましたところ、残していくと答えました。私が申し上げましたことは、アレクセイは総てわれらロシア人によってこの難渋に陥ったわけで、不憫にも覚悟をしていましたが、ただいまこの者だけを残し置き、いけにえとするようなことはあってはなりませんと申し聴かせました。同人の申し訳には書き置きを残すことがしかるべきと申し聴かせました。すなわちこれまでのご厚恩を感謝し、ならびにアレクセイは無罪の者であるので、何卒ラショワにお返しになられますよう願う趣

を私は認めましたが、その後いろいろ教諭し、これらの書面を焼き捨て、艦長に言ったこ
とには、今アレクセイの様子を見ての考えをアレクセイに聞かせたことはよかったとは思
います。私からアレクセイに言って聞かせ、いろいろ相談して、これまで二人で力を合わせ、
艦長の悪巧みをとどめさせてきたが、艦長の考えるところは分からないので、昼は私が気
を付け、夜はアレクセイが気を付け、両人が番人のようにして相談していましたが、その後、
艦長に言って聞かせたことは、逃亡は困難であるということでありました。その後、艦長
は毎回私もやりかたがよくないと言ってきましたので立腹も致しました。それでも私同伴
の者が悪事を企んでいることを日本人に告げることはできなかったのでございます。他に
引き留める方法もなかったのでこのように申し上げました。その後、ワシリエフへ私から
逃亡のことを申し出でました始末を話したところ、同人からシモーノフに伝達したこ
とを聞きました。その後、シモーノフが私へ聞かせたことには、牢屋の下を掘って逃亡す
るつもりとのことでございました。このことを私とアレクセイは気づきましたので、決し
てそのようなことにはならないと安心させました。しかしながら、みなみな、私のことを
疑いあるいは臆病者などと名付けましたが、ほかに方法もなかったので、そのように取り
計らっておりました。臆病などと言ったのは、私が考えるに、彼らは自分たちが思ってい
たところと違い、逃亡したが再び帰ってきて御役所に出たところが面目もなく恥辱を受け

62

て、自分から死ぬことを幸いと考えていたためでしょう。このように自分から死んだとす
れば無罪として牢中にあい果てても恥辱とはならないということでしょう。もし逃れ生き
延び死ななかった場合、恥辱ははなはだしいということになりましょう。こうして牢屋か
ら逃亡したものは「強情者」ということもできないとは思うところでございます。

私だけでなく、アレクセイも毎回、艦長らに言っていましたが、先だって提出いたしま
した願書、上申書など御奉行所はすべてお受け取りいただきました。そのなかで、神に誓っ
たこともございました。今、逃亡するなどという考えがあるならば、どうしてそのような
ことを書きますでしょうか。日本の御役人が日を追って御恩を示されているのにどうして
逃亡するのかと申し諭しましたが、彼らは一向に承知せず、只々今年ロシア船が私たちの
迎えとして来ても、私たちを見付けることが出来なければ、これを理由に戦争になるかも
しれないとのみ考え、とにかく悪い考えを去らせることが出来ず、いただきました御恩沢
や義理や道理を忘却してしまったのでございます。その後、艦長が私に申しますには、春
にもなるので、逃亡したらどうかと相談してきましたので、私は、逃亡は強いて考えてい
ませんと話しました。そして早いか遅いかは問題ではなく、私たちは理由を立てて話をし、
これまで願書や上申書等も御奉行所は御受け取り頂き、かつ御慈悲のことがらも増してい
るのになぜ逃亡するのかと説得しました。もし艦長が逃亡すれば、私の首をその贖いにし

たらいいでしょう。ただただ神の思し召しのままになすべきであり、死んだとしてもそれは覚悟していると話しました。艦長は、その時、私が逃亡に反対していることから、ともに逃亡することはやめると言いましたので私も少し安心いたしました。しかし、なおワシリョフに尋ねたところ、当時はだれひとり逃亡するとは考えていなかったようでした。そうしたところ当4月〔訳註：我が国の3月〕、御奉行所は一段の御恵みをもって、留置場所を取り換えになられまして、なおまたいくつかのお願いをお聞き届けになりありがたき幸せに存じました。ただ長くなんの仰せ付けもなかったので、心がけていたことがあれば言うように仰せ渡されたのでもあれば、善悪にかかわらず私の心中にあることを申し上げるだけと、日々仰せ渡されるのをお待ちしていたのみでしたが、一向に同伴の者たちは逃亡のことを言ってこなかったので、御番の衆や水夫や私にまでかくして、日々の食物を少しずつ蓄えていたことは御白州で彼らが申し上げた通りでして、一向に気づきませんでした。

4月中旬〔訳註：我が国の3月〕艦長が考えて言ったところは、「今年、ロシア船が来ることはあっても、日本側が私たちを引き渡すことにならなければ、戦争になることは必定にて、その場合は、またまた私たちは牢に入れられることになると思う。その時は何を楽しみにしたらいいのだろうか。やはり逃亡したほうがいいと思う」と私に言ってきました。それに対して私は、「戦争になるかならないかは分からないが、こののち牢に入れられる

64

ことはないと思う。かつ、たとえ逃亡したとしても島国であり、日本人は愚昧ではないので、すぐに逮捕され、その場合はどのような顔をして白州に座ったらいいものか。かつ、願書・上申書は誠実に書き上げただけでなく、神に誓ったことはどうするのだ」と申し諭しました。すると艦長は「今はまだ時期が早い。逃亡することはできない。かつその考えもない。しかしながら、憂鬱になってもよろしくない。逃亡することはできない。かつその考えもない。しかしながら、憂鬱になってもよろしくない。逃亡するところである」としました。そこで私は、「この期に及んで憂鬱になったとしても、自分は逃亡しない。ただただ神のみ心のままにと思う」と答えました。それは艦長も他の者も納得したことでありました。その後、またまた戦争の話になった時、私は「我々はなお、老衰の者ではなく、遅速は分からないが、日本人も自然と発展し、和睦になった時には再び故国を見ることもできる」と話しました。すると皆安心したようでした。実は私が人一倍安堵し、かつさらに考えて憂鬱というのではよほど時間もなく、そのうえ今申し聞かせたことを承諾したとのことですし、その後、時々申し聞かせたことには、彼らが表面的に悪心を改めたとしてしていたので、強いて心がけずにいましたところ、同月23日〔訳註‥我が国の24日に相当〕、他に行って帰ってきて、その夜、5つ時、全員が就寝しました。私はくたびれたので熟睡していたところ、翌朝、私とアレクセイが福松に起こされた時、ロシア人が逃亡したことを同人から聞かされました。驚きあわてて飛び起きてみました。もは

や後は空しくなったばかりで、実にこの時は狂人のようになり、同伴の者たちは私とアレ
クセイをだまして残したことは何とも申し訳がたく、このような恥辱はどのように申し
開きができるものかはわかりません。結局、先だってより彼らの考えは申し上げたように
思いもよらないもので、このようになったからは、私の不調法は恐れ入る次第でございま
す。この件でどのような罪科に処せられようとも申し訳もこれなく、また恨むようなこと
もございません。

　このたびこの書面を書き上げて呈上させていただきましたが、どうか先に提出させてい
ただきました上申書と照合してお読みいただけますようお願い申し上げます。私が考えま
すにいささかは相違するところもあろうかと思いますが、御奉行所においてよくよくお
考えいただけましたら、すべて同じ意味であり、ただ恥辱なこと〔岩下註：ゴローウニン
らが逃亡したこと〕は、お疑いを引き起こしたと言って省略しただけであり、ほかに悪心
がある人が増えるということも申し上げた通りでございます。しかし、悪心をいだいたと
いっても決して悪人ということではありません。ところが、入牢ということは追々承りま
したが、クリル人〔岩下註：アレクセイ〕が偽りを申し上げ、かつフヴォストフ乱暴の始末、
かつ日本が専らロシアを疑っているために、測量をしていたことを申し上げるのは心配が
ありましたのでこれまで申し上げていなかったのでございます。なおまた長崎においてレ

ザノフに申し渡されました件はとくと承知しておりましたので、決して国後に来て助けて
欲しいとお願いすることではありませんでした。

このことで私が申し上げました通り、彼ら〔岩下註：ゴローウニン一行〕が逃亡すること
ができなかったことや神のご加護によって皆無事に帰ってきたことは、私の憂い苦しむこ
とを除いても、まだ煩悶することをやめることができがたいものです。フヴォストフ乱暴
の件は、オランダ人がはなはだしく恨みを持ち、日本をしてロシアに懸念を持たせるよう
なことになり、そのうえこの度、同伴の者が逃亡することになり、なおなお長崎のオラン
ダ人が言うことに、これまでオランダ人を信用していなかった方々までも、ロシアは熊か
夷狄で、ロシアには義理も法もない国と考えてしまっていることだけが、私は苦々しく、
心苦しく思っている次第です。〔訳註：本文に熊か夷狄かと言っていることは、我が国が禽獣
同様だということと同じにてロシアでは慣用句になっている。もっとも凶暴な者のたとえで、ほ
かの猫や犬や狐、狸の類とも違うとのことである〕

御奉行所や御役人から厚い御恩沢を頂きながら、仇をなすようなことをいたしてしまい、
御慈悲を忘却したようなことになり、申し訳もございません。どのような人間もはなはだ
しい難儀に遭遇しなかった場合でも、胸の内の煩悶あるいは帰国することを昼夜忘れるこ
とができない心中などは理解できないものでございます。少々の難儀などは心中の思慮分

別もでるものですが、過度のことになってしまっては、格別の違いがあるものでございます。昼夜愁苦に沈み、その上、行く末も細くなってしまうことになって、思慮才智もぼやけてきて、ただただ昔や平穏だった日々が懐かしく、ますます豪昧になるばかりでございます。私たちのような難儀に遭遇した者だけがこのような心中を理解できるのでございます。私は壮年にあるだけで、彼ら〔岩下註：ゴローウニンら逃亡した者たちを指している〕同様のことをしなかっただけでございます。したがって、逃亡した同伴の者をもってロシア本国の人間を推量なさるのは、まったく違っています。ロシアは広大な地方をもっていますが、一国は一法をもって、遅速は分かりませんが、悪人がいれば処罰されるのでございます。ロシア人は熊ではございませんし、夷狄でもございません。人間に変わりはございいません。

ヨーロッパ地方でも実際、ロシアが軍隊のことに長じていることはよく知られていることでございます〔下げ札：ロシア本国が軍隊のことに長じているというのはムールが言っているだけであるが、別冊雪際亜ヒンランテユ合戦中、兵士が故郷に送った書簡の書き抜きの添え書きにこうしたことが書いてあると同人が言っている〕。すなわち1805年〔訳註：我が国の文化3年〕本国の将軍キニヤセ〔訳註：爵名〕ボクラチオナ〔訳註：姓名〕という者が8000人で駐屯していたところ、フランスが33000人で取り囲んでしまっ

68

た時、ボクラチオナが味方の軍勢に向かって「捕虜になるか、討ち死にするか、どちらか
しかない」と申し聞かせたところ、兵士たちは「ただ命令を待つのみです。死ぬことはか
ねて覚悟しています」という言葉とともにフランス軍に斬りかかり、味方も多く討ち死に
しましたが、ついにフランス兵20人を生け捕り、勝利し、本陣へ帰ってきたことがありま
した。〔訳註：本文にいう合戦とはネルマニア地方のことであるようだ。本陣というのはこの時
の総大将コトブフという者の本陣である〕これらは一端のことだけでございます。しかしな
がらこれらフランス人は戦争に関してよく鍛錬しており、なおかつロシアの士道が厳重に
行われていることは、かつて申し上げたカワワチョフが自殺したことも、レザノフの親類
でございましたので、レザノフが不埒な致し方をしたため、それを恥じて自殺したので
ざいます。このほかロシアには義理正実のことは実に称揚しております。かつ国法ではもっ
ぱら誠を推奨し、人を愛することだけでございます。他国では拷問なども今もって行われ
ているようですが、ロシアでは拷問は全く行われておりません。また法令の書中にある10
の有罪人を免じるというのは、これまで罪を犯したことがなく、一人の無罪の者を殺した
場合も処罰することをきちんと記しているのでございます。また人間の習い、若年の者の
心は蜜と蝋のたとえのようでございます。若年者への処罰はまた一段の憐憫をしないこと
でございます。以上でございますのでロシアの教法は数千年前より教法がある国に劣るこ

とはございません。ことにチエロウエコ○リュビウエエ○デニヤ〔訳註：これは病院や孤児院などの総称で、寡婦や孤独の者を養う役所である〕は、外国と比べれば、第一に多くございます。かつ諸々の芸術や技術、今日だんだんと発達していますので、諸外国に比べて遅れているということはございません。先年国王から日本に持たせた献上物をご覧になったと思いますが、これらは少しのもので、詳細はよく分かりませんが、もっとも私がこのようなことを申し上げても、日本では分からないかもしれませんが、外国人はどこにいてもよく知っていることでございます。かつ書籍も多く出版されておりますので、御奉行所に置かれましては、これらのことをよくお考えいただき、ロシアは夷狄なのか、熊なのか、御賢察くださいますようお願い申し上げます。追々ご吟味がありましたから、私は考えましたが、日本はロシアを殺人者または戦争を好む習俗のようにお考えのようですが、かつロシアが日本の北方の島をうかがい、奪い取ろうとする心がけがあるように思われていると思いますが、盗賊フヴォストフがやってきて、ますますご懸念が増したとは思いますが、さらにオランダ人がこのような心配を取り除くようにすべきなのに助長するようなことをしていると思います。これらはまったく大きな思い違いでございまして、なおまた、この度は私同伴の者が逃亡しまして、それがいいのだということも思い違いも同様のことでございます。しかしながらロシア本国は広大の考えを持ち、平和を愛することを同様に申し上げま

した。とても誤解を解くようなことはできませんでしたが、ただ道理を一通り申し上げました次第です。

ロシアが日本と戦争をすることに関して、その有利不利を比べて考えた場合、ロシアから蝦夷地を攻撃して占領することは事実に相違はないのですが、いよいよ占領してもどんな用に立つのかと思います。もし蝦夷地を保持しようとするならば、戦争中の経費や大勢を殺害するという損失を何をもって償うのでしょうか。また、その後、いろいろな場所に設置した要害の経費、そのほか守衛の士卒をはじめ、また守衛する士卒の輸送船の乗員などは辺境にして極寒の地で多くが死をまぬかれることはできないでしょう。ロシアの気候は寒暖の差がありますが、諸産物は多くが国内で産出し、かえって外国から望まれることがあっても、松前や蝦夷地諸島にどれだけ産物があるというのでしょうか。たいていカムチャッカで調達できるものばかりでございます。蝦夷地は多くの「悪魚」を産出し、ほかに昆布やアワビ、ナマコなどを産出しますが、カムチャッカでは少量の「善魚」を産し、蝦夷地等に送るほどもあるのです。昆布、アワビ、ナマコの類はロシアでは食用にはいたしません。このほか蝦夷地真珠を産出しますが、上記の粗悪な品はカムチャッカならびに第二島〔訳註：サセムンクの意味〕でたくさん産出します。イルカ、アザラシ、シカ、猫のようなテン、犬の

ようなキツネが少しいるだけですので、ロシアが狙うなどということはあるでしょうか。

カムチャッカ地方ではよいシカやテンなど１カ年で10万枚くらいは捕獲いたします。シカ

は各家々で多く飼育していますが、カムチャッカ地方などではロシア領分の中では至って悪地です

し、日本の蝦夷地もカムチャッカ同様の悪地な場所でございます。ロシア本国の各地は諸

産物の流通が自由でありますから、カムチャッカ地方などは一向に捨て置かれ、注意を払

われることもないので、どうしてロシアと日本が戦争をするようなことになりましょうか。

ロシアがクリル諸島や蝦夷地に来航するのは古代からのことで、日本人がその後だんだん

蝦夷地を日本に併合していったのでございます。それらのことはロシアに対し何の挨拶も

なかったのですが、ロシア本国では承知していたことでございます。さりながら、以上の

通り、貧石の諺をもって両国が戦争になるようなことになるのは好ましくありません。そ

うでありますから、今更なんの理由があってロシアがこの石を望んで合戦など仕掛けま

しょうか。日本の人々は蝦夷地の産物等は日本だけが知っているとお考えでしょうが、私

はすでに15年も前から知っておりまして、以上の通りでございます。〔訳註：本文で貧石と

言っているのは、蝦夷地が全く良質の産物がなく、実に一個の石同様であるので、貧乏な石とい

う意味で書いたのだとのことである。その下のこの石を望むというのも同様の意味である〕

　ロシア国中の者は熊あるいは夷狄ばかりではなく、善良な人間もいます。本国からの使

節〔岩下註：レザノフ〕に対して日本は不通の御回答になり、かつ、使節の従者や士卒まで自由を奪われましたが、本国にてはさっそく日本の真意を推察し、立腹することもございませんでした。中国人は自ら高慢で、日本が拒絶したようにロシア使節のガラハガロフキン〔岩下註：1805〜06年に中国に派遣されたゴロフキン使節のこと〕という者を拒絶したことがありましたが、本国諸役人は早速中国人の特異な点を悟り広大の心で恥辱を忍び嘆息したものです。中国と戦争することは幸運でもなく、雑事でもなく、しかしながら、中国人は早速厳命して、ロシア使節を拒絶した者を処罰したとのことです。〔訳註：本文に「日本の真意を推察し」とあるのは、前の方で書いていたようにロシアがヨーロッパからは遠隔の地にあるので国情が伝わりにくいということだと思われる。○本文に「中国人は自ら高慢で」とあることは、中国人は聖人が輩出した場所だと言うほか、諸国を夷狄と言ったりするのでこのように表現したのである。ロシア使節が交渉にのぞんだ場所は、イルクーツク近辺のキャフタという所で、ロシア人たちが利をむさぼったために双方が交易物に偽りを交えることが多くなり、ついにいったん交易を破談にした。今年、アレキサンデルが王位に就いた後、イルクーツク役人から再び中国に相互交易の条約を締結するため、条文を交渉する目的で、ロシア本国から本文にある役人が使節として北京へ向かう途中で中国人が遮った。このため使節はイルクーツクに派遣して、再び交易の条約中国人は厳命したのか、その後、中国の方から使節をイルクーツクに派遣して、再び交易の条約

を締結したことを聞いている。　難事でもないとのことで
ある。このキャフタからアムール川の南はテンの類が多く産出し、ことのほか上質である。この
ためこの地方を占領すれば、かなり国益にもなり、かつ地続きなので運送が容易で、全体雑事が
ないとのことを聞いた】

　去年ロシア国王の船旗が大いに恥辱を蒙った【岩下註：ゴローウニンらが日本側に囚われた】
ので、万が一、今年戦争になることがあっても、ロシア側に罪はないと思います。これま
で日本からご依頼はないのですが、本国の法律により、かつは人道的見地から、フヴォス
トフおよびダヴィドフの類も処罰しました。このように【岩下註：ロシアは】何事も寛
容の精神で対処しますが、その寛容にも限度があります。以上でございますので、私また
は同伴の者が国後に派遣されたのは、もしも本国より交戦の意図があって派遣されたのだ
としても、なんらかの理由があることでございまして、これら軍船も無事に帰国させるの
が宜しいと思います。しかし、本国の意図もよくわかりませんし、帰国の命令もありませ
んでした。　なお、私が考えますには、ロシアは戦争を好むわけではありませんが、日本側
が戦争を好まれるのだと存じます。【訳註：本文に船旗が大いに恥辱を蒙ったと言ったことは、
決して盗賊ではなかったのに盗賊の扱いを受けたこと、その上、艦長も召し捕らえられたので、
この上はこの船がどの港に入津しても帆柱のうえに船旗を上げることは不可能となった。もっと

74

も戦争になり船中で艦長が捕虜となり、または討ち死にしたら船旗を下げるのは致し方がないこ
とだ。このように国王の命名を受け、　船旗まで下付されたならば国王の恥辱となったのだと聞か
された〕

以上の件について、今よりのち、どのようなことがあろうとも、私が生存しているうち
はもちろん、死んだ後でさえも申し上げることは、嘘でないのですから、御責めください
ませんようにお願いします。　私が嘘を言っていないことは神のみぞ知ると思います。以上
でございますので私がこの書面を認めたのは、私ならびに同伴の者が帰国を命じられるこ
とを願ってのことではなく、ただこの書面を以て、日本側が西洋事情に通じることがなん
らかのお役に立つのではないかと思っただけでございます。私はロシアの武士で、もとよ
り夷狄ではございません。本来私の身は自由であり、本国の誠の道に従い、私同伴の者、
その地の者は勿論、その者の考えで分かりませんが、いささかのことをしたことを隠して
しまうこともやむを得ないことと思いますので、ただただ誠実に一通りのことを申し上
げたまででございます。これ以降どのようなことになろうとも、このこと〔岩下註：帰国〕
は願うものではございません。

私たちが御奉行所の広大な思し召し並びに御役人がそれをさらにご補佐されます思し召
しにも親しみ、心得て、そのうえでお願い申し上げますのは、日本がこれまでお考えになっ

てきたご心中をすべて除かれ、私どもロシア人も同じ人間とお考えくだされて、日本とロシアが隔たりなく交際ができるようにしたいと思いまして、恐れを顧みず、誠実に残すところなく書き上げました。もっとも私は先だってより御不審の趣を解きたいと思っておりましたので、善悪によらず、早くご命令くださいますようお願い申し上げます。〔訳註：この命令を早くもらいたいということは毎回話になり相違のないところである〕

そうしたところ、私同伴の者が逃亡し、帰国許可が下りないような状況となり、この度私はことごとく厳しく、御奉行所に申し上げました。先だって願書等認めました時は、帰国の許可を頂きたいということのみお願いいたしましたが、逃亡したことによりこのようなお願いはもはやできず、この度筆を執ったのは誠実一偏にのみ両国の幸福を考えてのことで、我が身を呈して、今、諸人の恥辱になることもこの書面にすべて書きましたので、私は〔岩下註：ロシアの〕士道も捨ててしまうことになりましたが、致し方もないことでございます。誠実に話しつくし死ぬよりほかございません。

私がこの度申し上げますことは、実に犯罪を犯した子供が、その父親に対して、生涯にわたって悪事を懺悔するような心持ちでございます。ただこれまでいただきましたご慈悲に対しての証として、ヨーロッパの事情を申し上げたく存じましてのことでございます。そのようにお考えいただけますようお願い申し上げます。

これまでいくつかお尋ねになられたことに対してそれぞれご返答を申し上げました

が、とかくご信用いただけていないようですので、私が考えましたところでは、これはオ

ランダ人が長崎で自分たちの利益のみ考えて、真実を覆い隠し、外国のことはことごとく

悪しざまに申し立てた結果と推察いたします。このオランダというのは先年イスパニアの

属国で〔岩下註：1556年スペイン領に編入、1648年ウエストファリア条約で独立承認〕、

両国は和同し助け合っていたし、そのうえオランダの法制はよく条理を尽くしたもので、

〔下札：本文の主旨を申し上げるのは、このところまでで、以下はヨーロッパの戦争に関

して申し上げる。〕オランダは堅固で他国の命令を一切聞くことなく、ヨーロッパにおい

ても人々が称賛し、小国ではあっても交易が盛んで海戦にもたけていて、地球上で領土を

拡大しているとのことです。いずれにしてもオランダの財力は計ることができないほどで

あるとのことでございます。ロシアの先帝ピョートルは英知のある人で、諸国を遍歴して

〔岩下註：1697～98年西ヨーロッパに大使節団派遣。ピョートル自身も随員として視察した〕

ついにオランダの方法を採用して、オランダを師と仰ぎ、この時から同盟し、不変を約束

するほどでありました。〔訳註：本文でオランダが以前ロシアと同盟を結んだと言っているこ

とであるが、ロシアはもともとオランダに恨みなどはなく、フランスがオランダを併合して、や

むなく敵国となったことを申し上げたようである。すなわちフランス国騒乱の趣ならびにオラン

ダがフランスに併合されたことはこれから申し上げることのようである〕

1791年から1792年〔訳註：寛政4、5年の時〕の間、フランスは騒乱状態であり
ましたから、ヨーロッパは大きな変革がございました。フランスは法制やキリスト教界、
国民など分裂状態となり、ついに1793年になってフランス国の国王と王妃を殺害しま
した。そこで、国王の親類や高官が仇を討とうとし、またそれまでの法制を擁護しようと
したものは皆々外国に逃亡しました。そのためさまざまな国が争うようになり、互いにフ
ランス国王を称したので、殺害することが止むことなく続き、ヨーロッパ諸国はフランス
の暴虐を憎むことになりました。どうにかして法制を再興したいと皆兵器を持つようにな
り、ついにフランス軍はゼルマニア〔岩下註：プロイセンのこと〕と戦争になりました。以下同じ〕、ペ
ルシャ、スペイン、イギリス、イタリアなどと戦争になりました。オランダも反フランス
に与しましたが、実に大河があふれ流れるごとく、小さな溝や川はたちまち押しつぶされ
ることにほかならず、フランスはこうした小国を併呑し、皆、フランスが恩を売り、ペル
シャは兵器を投棄し、スペインは和睦してフランスに味方し、イタリアはフランスの軍門
に降り平伏しました。しかしながら、オランダはなお戦争を継続しましたが、フランスは
天の助けを受けて、ついにオランダも倒れ、その財力も皆フランスに奪われました。その
後もオランダ国は戦争を好みませんでしたが、やむを得ずフランスのために戦争をするこ

とになったので、海外の領土〔岩下註：海外植民地〕ならびに船などは戦争となっても毎回勝利することが出来ませんでした。ゼルマニアはなお戦争を遂行したので次第に弱体化し、その際、ロシアと国境を接していたので、トルコならびにペルシャ・雪際亜等の国々より侵略されました。かつてハルニア国の者ども、フランスと同じく国王の位を望んだものがいたので、同国の領主はペテルブルクに逃亡するなどがございまして、いろいろ騒乱がございましたが、どれも鎮圧し、バイエルン国もロシアに屈服しました。そうしたところ1795年ゼルマニアやイギリスから救援要請があったので軍艦を派遣し、イギリスを防衛したことがございました。その際、フランスは、蘇亦斎亜〔訳註：地名〕ケレイエスキ島〔訳註：地中海にある島〕エギベツ〔訳註：アフリカ州にある〕ウエネチエ〔訳註：地名〕ことごとくアレスタブリカンスコエ〔訳註：その国は帝王がおらず、同盟一致の政治役所をたて、政治を執り行う呼び方である。かつてオランダ国の法は皆、この通りであったという。フランスの現在の帝王の名前はナポレオンと言い、ボストン人も同様である〕となりました。かつては身分の低い士官であったが、用兵術にすぐれた人であったので、ついに高官に上り、イタリアならびにエジプト地方で勝利し、帰国して、コンスウ〔岩下註：コンスル、執政、統領〕という第一等の官職に上り、名をナポレオン、姓をボナパルトと改めました。〔訳註：本文でコンスウという官名は、国王同様の権限があるけれど、同官は3人いて、国政を評議する

ことになっていた。先のボナパルトがこの官職になった時、ほかの2人は、まったく愚鈍な者で
あったので、ボナパルトが皇帝になった後は、この2人は貴族に〔した〕とのことである〕

以上の状況で、ヨーロッパ全体が疲弊したためロシアに救いを乞うことになり、先主バ
ウェウペトロウイチ〔訳註：現主の父〕が、1797年、国中の兵士を動員して、大将な
らびに官名ヘウジマルシヤリ執政ガラハスオロフという者にフランスの侵略を防がせまし
た。この者はゼルマニア、イタリアならびに蘇亦斎亜等の地に侵攻したフランス軍を撃退
し、1799年、ペテルブルクに凱旋しました。かつまたその際、ケレチエスキハという
島をフランスが占領したので、これをロシア本国に要請して「本島を奪回しました。この島の領主の名前は、デ
ルシトといい、ロシア本国に要請して「本島を防衛してほしい」と言ったので防御のため
の軍船を差し遣わしました。〔訳註：本文に言うケレチエスキハに最初に赴いた将軍の名前は
ウシヤコウという者で、その後交代した。シニヤウインという者が赴いたとのことである〕

その際、オランダ人ブリンチア〔訳註：ロシアの大名の通称である〕名前ヲランスカコと
言う者ならびにイギリス人からともに要請があって、軍船を派遣し、オランダを救援し、
ケウデルン〔訳註：地名〕という場所を占領して、船でイギリス人がフランスを打ち破り
ました。そうしたところ、この時、ロシアもイギリスも地理不案内な状況だったので、ゲ
ルマン〔訳註：ロシア軍の将軍〕という者がフランスの捕虜となっていました。それより、

アリキマル〔訳註：地名〕という場所を占領したけれども、段々とフランスとフランスの仕業でオランダの味方が心変わりをして、オランダ国民はこのブリンチアならびに異国人を支援することを嫌うようになり、その後どのようなこともはじめの本意が実現しないような状況になってしまいました。そのため、上記ブリンチアならびにジュカ〔訳註：官名である〕ヨルカスコ〔訳註：イギリス軍将軍である〕という者が指揮して、多くの人間を殺害し、財貨を費やしたが、やむを得ずオランダ国を見捨てて帰国することになりました。イギリスも同じようなことになりました。〔本文の戦争の時、ムールは16歳で、総司令官チチェコフという者の軍船に乗り組み、船中の運用に従事したため、戦争行為はしなかったが、戦争は直に見たとのことである〕

その際、イギリス人はマルツ〔訳註：この島は地中海にあるとのことである〕〔岩下註：マルタ島のこと〕という島を占領しました。これにより諸国の食料補給路が確保されたため、フランス人はやむを得ずこの島をイギリスに引き渡した。ここからイギリス人は段々フランス人をエジプト地方に追い払い、かつ海上戦でたびたび勝利を得たので大いに高慢になり、古来よりの海上習俗をすべて軽んじて、各国の船を拿捕するようなことを致しました。〔訳註：本文の海上習俗というのは、これまでヨーロッパの慣習では敵国の船は拿捕しても、そのほかの、敵国でない国の船は拿捕されることがなかったが、イギリスは最近新法を制定して、

たとえ、敵国の船でなくとも敵国に向かう船ということであれば、すべて拿捕するとのことである〕

1799年マルタ島領主デリタという者がペテルブルクへやってきて、この島をロシアに編入して防禦してほしいと要請してきました。そこでフランスはじめヨーロッパ諸国に相談したところ、了解を得ることができましたので、イギリスにロシアがこの島を領有すべきとその際申し送りました。そのほかには、小国などと軽視するようなことなく、また敵国でない船ならば拿捕されることがないということも申し送りました。またマルタ島をロシアが領有することを申し送りました。ところがイギリス人はこの命令を受けいれることができなかったので、戦争になると返答したのでした。そうしたところ、バウエルベルトウイチが、1801年初春に頓死したので、ミロリユビウイ・アレキアントル・バウロウイチが〔訳註：現ロシア皇帝〕位に即いたところ、早速イギリス軍船がコペンハーゲン〔ターニア国の首都〕にやってきて、ターニア〔岩下註：デンマーク〕の無防備な場所を攻撃して戦争になりました。イギリス軍は大人数でしたが、デンマークが厳重な防禦体制をとるまで、デンマークの「プリンチヤ」〔訳註：この国の大名のような者の通称。〔岩下註：プリンスのこと〕〕が広大の取り計いをして、すべて休戦となったのでございます。〔本文のロリユビウイ〔岩下註：本文ではミロリユビウイ〕というのは、和睦を好むものという意味で、この

82

アレキサンドルが即位したのちはヨーロッパ諸州が平和になる場合は、このアレキサンデルが取り扱ったり和睦を促したりした。このため、ヨーロッパ全州から名をこのように唱えられたのである。〔〇本文のデンマークのプリンチヤという者は、デンマーク王の嫡子の意味で、広大の取り計いとは、イギリス大船二艘がデンマークの城郭に進出してきたとき、遠浅の海で進退窮まったので城中から厳しく鉄砲を打ちかけた。そこでイギリスから使者を派遣し、イギリス軍船の中には最近生け捕ったデンマークの船員が多く乗り込んでいるので、この船を破壊するとこのデンマーク人捕虜が全員死亡することになると申し送った。かくしてこの二艘の軍船が撃沈すればイギリス軍は全く敗軍になりかねない状況だったのだが、このプリンチヤが自国の乗組員というこ

とに欺かれ、鉄砲による攻撃を中止させたので、イギリス軍船は少々破壊されたにとどまり、退却することができたので、敵味方ともにプリンチヤの慈悲心に感心して、休戦になったとのことである〕

ロシア皇帝はこの様子を聞いて、使者をイギリスに派遣して言うには「平和に暮らすのは戦争をしないことだ」としましたので、イギリスはついにデンマークならびにシウエシエユ〔岩下註：スウェーデン〕と和睦し、ロシアより水や食料を供給され帰国しました。寛容で広大な心の持ち主である皇帝なので、「唯一島」〔訳註：マルタ島の意味である〕のために大人数が失われる〔岩下註：多くの人命が失われる〕のを恐れ、ついに属島同然のマル

夕島をイギリスに譲りました。その後、ヨーロッパ諸国に要請して全体に和睦するように労をとりました。そうしたところ、イギリスとオーストリア等が会合して、最終的にフランスとの和睦を議して定めました。こうしてヨーロッパ全土がアレキサンデルの徳を称揚しました。こうしてさまざまな海の港には皆々交易船のみが多く渡海し、皆々歓楽し安堵して暮らすことができるようになりました。貧乏人も〔岩下註：食べられるだけ食べることができ〕飽きることを知らないような状況でした。なお、戦争が終わらない時、フランス人は和睦の書面を認めて条約を締結しました。以前のようにオランダ・イタリア・カノウエル〔訳註：国名〕などそのほか占領されていた地方もすべて元通りにするということを書いておりました。それでイギリスと同様に地球上さまざまなところに存在する占領地を引き取ったところ、フランスがこの条約の通りに引き渡さなかったのでございます。和睦するもますます出張の場所等〔訳註：オランダ・イタリアなどのことを意味する〕を警護し、またやむを得ず戦争を始めるに至りました。1804年には諸地方の戦争で血が流れましたが、まるで血の川にもなったようなところがございました。ロシア皇帝はこの様子を見るに忍びないことだと言い、大いに苦心して再び新たにフランスとイギリスの和睦の仲介の労をとりましたが、一向に整いませんでした。フランスはヨーロッパ全土を併合することだけを考えていたので、自国の親類の者または同盟の国々〔訳註：プロイセン・オースト

リア・雪際亜などのことであるとのこと〕のため、かつ目指していたところと齟齬をきたしたので、ロシアも兵器を握って戦争をせざるを得なかったとのでございます。〔本文にフランスはヨーロッパ全土を併合することだけを考えていたということは、次第に刊行された書籍もあり、申し上げるまでもないのだが、まったく5世界を併合するという考えで、ロシアと和睦したのち、フランスより申し送ったことには、どうにかして国中にある道路を借り受けて、大軍を黒海に差し向け、アジア地方を侵食したいと言っていたが、ロシアは承知せず、そのような展開はしないことになった。前文にある通りアフリカ地方へはニエギヘツが討たれ亡くなり、また、ヨーロッパ全土和睦した場合、軍船を多く建造し、アメリカ地方を併呑する考えであったので、イギリス軍船を拿捕するだけで戦争になった。そのため、全くヨーロッパ全土に限ったことではなく、5世界併呑の考えではあるが、実にその量を知らないことで、申し上げても却ってご信用いただけないこともあるかと思い、ヨーロッパ全土とのみ認めたことであるとのこと〕

　この時分、フランスの第一頭領〔岩下註：ナポレオンのこと〕は皇帝の位につき、その兄弟をオランダやイタリアの諸侯に任じました。そして、1805年ロシア軍将軍ケネラウアンシエフ〔訳註：役名〕コトソフという者がオーストリアへやってきて、またプロイセン王国を経てウイーン〔訳註：オーストリアの首都〕へやってきて、オーストリアの考えや

ロシアとオーストリアの将軍が不和であることなどをフランスが推察して、先にオーストリアを打ち破り、数万人の人数にてロシア軍を取り囲みました。ここでロシア軍は惨敗し、たくさんの軍勢・大砲・兵糧を失い、最終的に戦場に踏みとどまっただけでありました。

この時、フランス軍の総司令官は皇帝ナポレオンでございましたが、両軍合わせて約10万人が一気に戦死しました。ロシア軍の戦死者は2万6千人でございました。そうしたところオーストリアが要請したことには、ロシアがオーストリアを見捨てて帰国しないのであれば、ナポレオン皇帝はいずれとも和睦しないとのことですから、どうか帰国してほしいとのことであったのでロシア軍は帰国したのでありました。そうしたところ、オーストリアの首都ウィーンというところの財宝類はすべてフランスに強奪され、フランチアフトロイ〔訳註：オーストリア国王の名前〕は難儀の和睦を果たし、これまでリムスカコ帝と唱えていた位をおとして、アフシラリスカコ〔訳註：オーストリアの異名〕か、またはオーストリア帝と唱えるようになりました。〔本文リムスカゴと言うのはオーストリアの近辺の国数十を合わせてムスカコ同盟と唱え、ゲルマニアがこの諸国の皇帝となっているということである〕

かつ、国中レイレスカコ同盟と唱える大名のような者がいて、これまた分割してフランスに与して多くの領土を失いました。このようにフランスが段々勝利が多くなって、各地

を侵略する欲望が強くなっていったので、プロイセンに対しイギリス・ロシアが少しも侵略しないということになりました。それゆえ、1806年の夏、ナポレオンという者がプロイセンを打ち取って来年の正月はモスクワ〔訳註：ロシアの旧首都、我が国にてはムスコヒアと言ってきたところである〕にて春を迎えるということを送ってきました。これによりロシア国内の兵力を分割して、その勢いを弱めようと、このナポレオンはトルコ・ペルシャ・中国等に使者や贈り物等を送って、ともにロシアと戦争をしてほしいと申し送ったのでございます。軽薄のトルコやペルシャはなんの考えもなく直ちにナポレオンに与しましたが、中国がフランスに答えた主旨は「昔ロシアと和睦をしたが、総じて闘論〔岩下註：紛争〕になったことはなく、和睦の書面を今破ることはない。どんな理由で中国から戦争を仕掛けるのか」ということでありました。

そうしたところ、トルコやペルシャはロシアより義理をもって次第に教諭しましたが、一向に取り用いることはなかったので、アレキサンドルもついに怒って一緒に武器を取ろうと言いました。そうしたところ、ヨーロッパ全土の軍隊がプロイセンに集結し、ただオーストリアだけが追手の激戦に疲れ果て、戦争の道に至ることを恐れ出陣しなかったのです。こうしてロシア軍も1802年プロイセンの援軍としてプロイセン東国境に出張し、その地を守ることとなりました。プロイセン軍は全員プロイセンの西国境に張り付きました。

そうしたところ、フランス・オランダ・イタリア・イスパニア・蘇公斎亜・波羅厄亜の諸軍が一度に押し寄せて、実に、大海の大波の中の弱々しい小船のような状況で、プロイセンの先代王が調練した壮強の軍隊も一飲みになり、エナ【訳註：プロイセン王国中の地名】という所の近辺で煙や霧が消え去るように敗亡しました。このようにプロイセンのほかは援軍もなく、国中皆々恐怖し屈服して、国人皆々村落や都市を遺棄してロシアまたはオーストリアに逃亡して国中が空虚になりました。兵糧や馬に至るまでことごとくフランスに奪われたので、領主は車を使って、ゲニギッベルク【訳註：プロイセンの地名、ロシア国境に近く】へ逃れ、それよりフランス軍がロシアに迫ってきました。ロシアの将軍は初めは

【訳註：役名】ヘルジマルシヤウ・ガラフ・【訳註：姓名】カメンツケイという者がいました。この人は病気だったので【訳註：役名】ケネラフアンセフ・ガラフ・【訳註：姓名】ベニンキセンという者が将軍になり、少々の戦闘はその数も分かりません。フウトスカマエシイシシユエイラウ・ゲンギツベルク【訳註：皆、地名である】近辺にて三回の決戦がありました。その際、三度ともロシアが勝利したが、士卒は大半が討ち死にしました。フランスならびに同盟諸国軍の死亡人数は、およそロシア軍の４倍余りだということです。これによりロシアは食料が不足し、馬もすべて撃ち殺され、その上道路が劣悪で、本国まで帰れたものはほとんどいなかったのです。【本文の道路が劣悪というのはこの地方は雪解けになると

88

一円に沼地になり、なかなか通行することができず、酷暑の中か、積雪の時節に通行することができるということである〕

そうしたところ、フランス側は戦争当初より所どころでプロイセンの倉庫など略奪したので兵糧も余裕がありました。こうしてロシア人は飢え、そのうえ八方から攻め込まれたため、あちらこちらに奔走して決戦となり、疲労ははなはだしく、ヒリデランデ〔訳註：プロイセンの国の中の地名である〕のあたりでの決戦では、敵味方の負傷者、疲労者がはなはだしく、双方互いに引き取ることさえできない状態でありました。〔訳註：この時は両軍ともに戦いに疲れただけで引き取ることも出来ない状況であった〕この時初めてかのナポレオンはこのありさまを見て、ロシアからすべて勝ちを得ることができないことを思い知って、かつトルコやペルシャ等が頼みにならないことを承知したとのことでございます。

トルコは少々闘争がありましたが、一向に弱々しいやり方で、この節の戦争にモウグイエ〔訳註：地名〕ならびにドナヤ〔岩下註：モルダヴィアならびにドナウ地方〕という川があ

る地方を失いました。〔訳註：ロシアがこの地方を切り取った〕ペルシャはバキンスリエ〔訳註：地名〕そのほかたくさんの領地を失い〔訳註：これまたロシアが切り取ったものである〕敗走しただけで、まったく合戦はなかったのでございます。〔訳註：この合戦は前書きの合戦とはまた別の合戦で、トルコ・ペルシャの両国は双方を侵略し

たので、〔役名〕ヘルチマルシヤウ〔姓名〕クドウイフというものがプロイセンに赴き、トルコ
へは〔役名〕ケネラウアンセーラ〔姓名〕ミーセリソン〔姓名〕同断〔姓名〕ブクセデンという
者が、両人ともそれぞれ立ち向かい、勝利を得たという。別の合戦では前文にあるようにフラン
スから要請されたとされ、かつ両国が助けにならないことをナポレオンが承知していたという証
にこのことを前文に認めたのである〕

〔下げ札：本文でドナウ地方を占領した後、軍中の士官が故郷に送った書簡がロシアで発
行された新聞のなかに記されているので、翻訳して別冊に差し上げることとする〕

ナポレオンはロシアに面会したいと要請し〔訳註：エヒリデヲンデ合戦の翌日のことである〕
面会したところ、和睦の件を申し談じ、大いにロシアの自由になって和睦が定まった。〔本
文にあるロシアの自由とは、ペルシヤ国王がすでに敗走しているのでこの地方はすべてフ
ランスが掠めとったが、プロイセン国王に元の通りこの地方を返すならば、和睦すること
はできない。そうであるならばなお戦争することになるとアレキサンデルが言った。この
ためフランスは承諾したとのこと。その他フランスが占領した土地を分割して、ロシア皇
帝に与え、またはイギリスの内密の書面等をフランスが奪って、アレキサンデルに贈り示
すなどということになった。〇この和睦は、則ち彼らが本国出帆の年で、前文にあったフ
ルシイアより帰国し、カナンシタと申す者は、この和睦が済んで帰ることになった〕

イギリスはかねてロシアと同盟をしていますが、前々よりロシアばかり艱難辛苦の決戦となり、自分自身としてはイスパニア・フランス・オランダ等の遠方にある領分が奪われるだけでございます。ところが、ロシアは近年、イギリスとの交易のやり方を変えてみたのです。【訳註：これは先年イギリス人に限り国中どこまでも入り込んで、我がままに交易をするようになった。それゆえアレキサンデルが皇帝になったあと、こうした交易のやりかたの変化を把握し、ペテルブルクの港のみにて国中に入れ込み、買いだしは差し止めとなった】

また候、この度フランスに和睦を申し入れたことを立腹し、ついにロシアならびに同盟のデンマークの合戦に及んだということです。デンマークの備えがないところを襲い、諸国和睦になるまで、領主の船にすべてイギリスに受け取らせたく申し聞かせていたが、デンマークが承知しなかったので、首都を半分焼き払い、デンマークはやむを得ず、船ならびに軍装の諸品をイギリスに与えたとのことである。【訳註：このデンマーク合戦のことは、ジアナ号がこの度の海路で観たコペンハーゲンの戦いである】

雪際亜【岩下註：スウェーデン】の国王は年若で、戦争を好んだので、実に不都合なことを仕組んだりして、フランスのために遂にポメラニア【岩下註：ポンメルン】という領地をすべて失いました。ジアナ号が今回海路で大砲の音を聞いたのは、すなわち、このフランスのスラタラズント【岩下註：シュトラルズント】、ポメラニア【訳註：すべて雪際亜

の領地の地名である）の城郭を打ち破った時の合戦の時でございました。ロシア国皇帝は

クスタフ〔訳註：雪際亜の国王の名前である〕〔岩下註：グスタフ４世〕と親類であったので、

たびたびこのような戦争になるのを回避するようにしていました。もしやめなければつい

に戦争になって国を失うことを申し諭していましたが、それは喜ぶべきことでありますが、

短気の国王が遂に命令して、ロシアの使節を召し捕って牢獄に収監し、かつ使節の居宅中

を捜索して、文書類をすべて印刷して公開しました。〔訳註：本文の使節は、前文にあるも

ので、同盟の国々に派遣された使節である。この者の居宅にあった文書類は、実にロシア皇帝の

内密の文書もあったが、それを刊行したので、大いにロシアの恥辱になったということである〕

これは使節の恥辱だけでなく、すべてロシア皇帝の恥辱でありますが、広大な心のアレ

キサンドルは雪際亜の使節を招き〔訳註：これまた平常からペテルブルクに駐在していると

のことである〕、言って聞かせたことには、「その方の国王に対しては、何事も篤く取り扱っ

てきたのに、その方の国王は不届きのやり方でもって報いてきた。かつ恥辱を与えられて

も、予もそのように取り計らうのかとその方は案じることはない。何事もその方の考え次

第に致し、我が国に居住したいのであれば居住するがよいし、帰国したければ、いつでも

その方の考え次第である。予が思うところは、ただその方の国王が安全であることだけを

思っているので、この度フランスと和睦したことは、今回恥辱を与えられたことも予は忘

92

却することにしたい。それなのでこの旨をその方より国王に報告せよ」とのことでした。

この使節が帰国したとき、護送の役人が例の通り雪際亜へ帰って国王に願い出ました。国王クスタフは若年でありましたので、さっそくこの使節も収監され、かつイギリスにわいろを贈り、ともにロシアと戦争をしてもらいたいと申し遣わしました。それからロシアはついに雪際亜のヒュランデュ〔訳註：地名〕コツランデマンという島ならびにスウエアホルグ〔岩下註：ストックホルム〕、アホフ〔訳註：地名〕などというところを占領しました。

ロシア国のみならず、雪際亜国中の者もこの国王のよろしくないことを思いあたっていたので、国中の者が国王の叔父プリンチヤマンランドスカコ〔訳註：名前〕という者を国王に立て、若年の国王は位を退くので、どうかロシア国王におかれては和睦していただきたいとお願いしました。すなわち一八一〇年にロシアは和睦し、占領していたスウエアポルグ、アボフの二か所を残してそのほかはすべて返還しました。また多くの食料を贈ったといいます。〔本文雪際亜国のことであるが、食物入手が不自由な場所で、このような戦争があったため、スウエアボルク、アボフの二か所を占領したので、このように食料を送ったのである〕

〔下げ札：本文ユンランテテユを占領したことは、この時の軍士ボルユという者より故郷に贈ったロシアの新聞のなかにあるかもしれないので、すなわち別に抜き出して翻訳し差

し上げることとする〕

コペンハーゲンでのイギリスのやり方が甚だ不届きでしたので、ロシアは大いに立腹したのですが、イギリスと合戦の書面を取り換えたところ、この書面ともに、ロシアから来ていた商人や職人に限らず、そのほか船々交易の諸荷物や家屋敷に至るまで、今より6か月以内に諸始末をつけ、イギリスに引き取るように、6か月の間は猶予を与えると申し渡したのでございます。またロシア商人にも申し渡しがありました。イギリス人には6か月の猶予の後、帰国を申し渡しましたので、これまでの商売の取引を完済し、それぞれ役人を張り付けることでございます。〔訳註：本文コペンハーゲンにてイギリスがやり方が不届きだという

のは、前文にあったデンマークの船ならびに軍隊の装備品を奪いっとったことである。デンマークはロシアの親類国で、イギリスもこの時同盟国であった。そうしたところ備えが十分ではないところを見込み、わがままなやりかたをしたので、ロシアは立腹したのである〕

1807年より1811年までの間、厳しい戦争はなかったと思います。イギリスがボルチモア港にてスベシネイ〔訳註：ロシアの官船の名前である。ジアナ号が同港に入津した時、滞留していた船である〕を奪い取ったこと、そのほか、レウエリア〔訳註：港名〕の近辺でヲベナ〔訳註：ロシア官船、一本マストの小船である〕が大砲わずか14門のところ、計

94

らずもイギリスの大船、大砲48門積の船に出会い、しばらく海戦になりました。兵士が多く殺害され、船中の役人が九死に一生の傷を受けたことなどがありましたが、みな大きな戦争ではありませんでした。ロシア官船大砲74門積の船がバウチイスカ〔訳註：海名〕〔岩下註：バルチック海〕のホルグ〔訳註：港名〕というところの近辺でイギリス船二艘に追われ、一艘はロシア船よりも大船であったが、しばらく海戦しました。そして、人数が半数以上撃ち殺され、かつ帆を破られてしまったので、その船はとうとう岩礁に打ち上げられ動けなくなってしまったため、船中の乗組員は上陸し、船を焼き捨てました。イギリス人は上陸しなかったとのことでした。〔訳註：本文軍船のことは、ジアナ号が出帆してからのことで、カムチャツカにて知ったことだと聞いた〕

フランスとロシアの和平が締結されましたが、すべてうまくいったわけでもありません。すなわちウエシチフツムミ、ウエムチエムベルカ、サキソニア、ハワリヤ〔訳註：皆地名である〕などの場所にフランスから大名のような者を派遣しました。そのほか、ウエネナム〔訳註：地名〕、熱児瑪泥亜国〔岩下註：オーストリア〕のアテリアチチエスコムという海岸地方、イタリアのアリムスクエヲブラシチ〔訳註：地名〕の諸国は皆フランスに併呑されました。それよりリム〔訳註：イタリアの地名〕という場所をフレーム・コロトーム〔訳註：第2国という意味である〕と名付け、オランダは悪いところがあるので、はじめ半分を

管理し、半分をオランダと称していたが、その後、またまた全部を併呑しました。アムステルダム【訳註：オランダ第一の都である】をテレチームコーロドム【訳註：第一の都という意味である】とフランス皇帝は命名しました。

【本文にオランダは悪いところがあるという意味は、はじめフランス皇帝の弟〔岩下註：ルイ・ナポレオン〕を国王に即位させたが、この弟がフランス皇帝の考えとは異なる政策をとったため、フランス皇帝は大いに怒り、はじめに領国の半分を取り上げ、その後、全国を取り上げたとのこと。かつ本文二都のことは、第二、第三ということで、みな自国とする証拠とのことである。第一はフランス国都を第一としたのことである】

波児杜尾里亜、伊斯把泥亜等の地方にイギリスから援助がありましたが、ついにフランスに占領され、この支援は無駄になったということでございます。このアリムスクエ領主ならびに伊斯把泥亜領主らは、現在フランス国内に居住し、波児杜尾里亜領主はブラシリアへ敗走したのでございます。熱児瑪泥亜国はその国土を削減されることを嫌い、残兵を集めてフランスと決戦をしましたが、一日で両軍合わせて15万人が戦死するということも
ございました。大戦争でフランスと決戦をしましたが、熱児瑪泥亜国軍の将軍が二心あるものばかりだったので、フランスは大敗北を免れついに和平を結び、熱児瑪泥亜国王ラランチャトロイの娘をもってフランス皇帝の妃として婚姻することとなりました。私が最近知ったことでは、

96

このナポレオンはまたまたロシアと戦争をするつもりであるということですが、その後は神妙にふるまっているとのことです。アレキサンドルはひとたび和平に同意することはないと思います。

ありますが、もし戦争になったならば容易に敗北することはないと思います。

これらのことは忘れないように書き記したものでございます。しかしながら、少々の手落ちや年月日等の書き損じもあるかもしれません。どうか御推察ください。まったく書籍や覚書もなく、全体暗記していたことばかりです。さりながら虚偽などのことは一語もなく、実に太陽のように、遅速なく、雲や霧を払って、なお新しい光をあらわすようなものだと思います。

この書面をもって疑いの筋を説いていただき、かつ、ロシアが戦争を好むというお考えをやめていただきましたら、たとえ私はここで死んでも本望であり安心していくことができます。　先年、ロシアが使節〔岩下註：レザノフ派遣のこと〕を派遣したことはまったく同盟を結びたかっただけで、ただただ交易を行って、富を蓄えたいというだけではございません。堅く条約を結んだら、両国の国民は御互いに発展するでしょう。そうでありますから、交易を願ったのは銅などを貪るような考えはありません。日本は双方にもある産物が豊富で、ロシア国東地方〔岩下註：広くシベリアを指す〕は全体産物がなく、ただ美鹿の皮類がたくさんあるだけです。日本にはこうしたものが不足しているということですので、これ

がロシアより日本に交易を願う基本的な考えです。そうしたところ、その故か、日本はロシアを悪者とし、いかなることも許可できないとのお答えを頂き、レザノフへの返答などは実に私どもも理解できないものでございます。

〔本文に銅を貪るということは、まったくオランダが日本銅を貪って持っていくことを聞いているので、書いて注意喚起したとのこと。書面でオランダのことを全体悪しざまに避難しているのが本意であるわけではなく、このように書いたことが十分あるということのようである〕

　日本の上位の方々が、私の申し上げました言葉を不信に思われましても、ご心配になられるようなことはございませんので、御役人を1人か2人、ロシアに派遣していただき、すべてご尋問いただけましたら、事実は早々に判明いたします。御役人がロシアに赴かれましたら、捕らえられて、獣をいれる牢のようなところに押し込められ、ご苦労をおかけしたり、命を縮めるようなこともあるかもしれないなどとお察しになられるかもしれませんが、そのようなことはございません。ロシアにおいてはこのようなことはいたしませんし、ただただ外国人には親切にすることが習俗で、日本人が1人でも牢獄で死ぬようなことはございません。

　ロシアの民衆の諺にプラウタ・グワザ・コヲレチ、誠に・眼を・突、ということがあり

45.

ますけれど、この諺は、小さい者にはかなうこともあるけれども、広大の思し召しの人に
はそういうことはないと思います。私の主人〔訳註：アレキサンドルのことである〕は年若
き頃、馬を好みました。ある時、思わずこの馬が暴れ、逸仕国主が落馬しました。そうし
たところ通りかかりの農民がこの馬を捕らえ、大いに立腹してこの馬を殴り、国王の傍ら
に引いてきて言うことには、「国王がどうしてこのような馬に乗られるのですか、こんな
馬だから傷も出来ないのです。まったく悪い心がけではないでしょうか。国王が良馬を持っ
ていらっしゃらないというのなら、我々が買ってでも進呈いたします。願わくは御身を大
切になさってくださいませ。」と言うのであった。アレキサンデルはその親切に感謝し、
直ちに馬を取り換えたとのことである。

〔訳註：本文に言う「誠に眼を突く」という俗諺の意味は、真実のみ申告する場合には、かえっ
て人を突くようなことで、まさに今いさめられるという俗語ということである。そうしたところ
が、心が広大の人に至っては、このようなことがなく、アレクサンドルのように誠心から感謝す
るのである。この書面の中に失敬な言葉が多くあると思うが、広大の思し召しを以て、誠実なと
ころだけを御聴き取り下されたくという意味を含んでいるのだということである〕

私はすでに棺桶に臨んでいるようなものではございますが、〔岩下補足：いいかげんなこ
とを〕申し上げることはございません。御聞き苦しいところはあろうかとは思いますが、

99　ムールによる獄中からの上申書　上下

お許し下さいますようお願い申し上げます。これ以上に私が願うことはございませんが、万が一お聞き届け下さるようなことがございましたら、三つのお願いがございます。その第一はこの書面を写しにて後ほどロシアに送致していただきたく、第二は二重に難を受けたアレクセイならびに私同伴の者に対する厳しい取り扱いを免じていただきたい、第三は今回私は処罰されるか、または病人という扱いになるのか分かりませんが、そうであってもどうかこの貧しい言葉〔岩下註：ムールの上申書〕をお焼き捨てになられませんように、これだけをお願い申し上げます。

1812年6月我が国5月　ロシア皇帝の士官　ムール

ロシア軍艦ジアナ号乗組員人名簿　1807年イユリヤ7月〔訳註：我が国6月頃〕25日〔この本文あるカランシターツ〔岩下註：クロンシュタット〕出帆の時、乗り組みの人数を報告しますので、すなわち7月25日と記しました〕

〔訳註：役名〕甲必丹　　　　　　　〔訳註：名〕ワシレイ　　〔訳註：姓〕ゴローウニン

同　　　　　　　　　　　　　ヘートル　　　　　イリコルド

レイチヤナンド　　　　　　　ヒヨトル　　　　　モウル

同　　　　　　　　　　　　　イリヤ　　　　　　ウルタコウ

100

レイチマナ	シミテーレ	カルタフチヨフ
【註記：カムチャッカで死亡した】		
同	フセーヨウ	ヤクーシキン
同	ニカンドル	ヒラトフ
シツルマン	アンデレー	ハレブニコウ
ムワチイシツマン	ワシレイ	ノウーキイ
同	ワシレイ	スレツニイ
エレカリ	ボクダン	ブラント
ペリヂイル	ウハヂンメル	スコロヅモフ
コンスタアベン	フエドド	バベリン
ビサリ	ステバン	サウエリエフ
コミサア	エリザル	ナチヤビンスキイ
ポヂキボル	エゴル	イリイン
【註記：1809年、アフリカで死亡した】		
クワルデルノエシテル	エゴル	サウエリエウ
同	イワン	ボリシヤコフ

同　　　デシヤチニカ　　　イワン　　　　　サウエリエフ

同　　　　　　　　　　　　　ダニコ　　　　ラブチン

〔註記：一八〇九年、タナニで死亡した〕

ハルシニカ　　　ステバン　　　マテルシヤノフ

シレサレ　　　　ヂミイテレ　　アラズドブルデン

クジニヤチカ　　ヒョードロ　　ヒョードロフ

コノバチカ　　　イワン　　　　スチコフ

クボル　　　　　アレフエイ　　シチエヅリン

〔註記：一八〇〇年、カムチャッカで死亡した〕

カノエル　　　　イワン　　　　フエドロフ

同　　　　　　　アンドラチエ　ボートフ

同　　　　　　　ニキホル　　　キレボフ

同　　　　　　　チイハン　　　イレンチエフ

マタロス　　　　デミイラレ　　シイモノフ

同　　　　　　　シハイル　　　シカエフ

同　　　　　　　キリコリ　　　ワシリエフ

同　シヒリドン　マカロフ

同　イワン　トロフ

〔註記：1809年、カムチャッカで死亡した〕

同　ペートル　アンデレトフ

同　ペートル　イワノフ

〔註記：1810年、カムチャッカで死亡した〕

同　エリセイ　ブルチヨフ

同　キリゴリ　アレキサンドロフ

同　イワン　シシヨノフ

同　セリゲイ　サウエリエフ

同　ウエシユキク　ヒラトラ

同　マエトロ　ヲロジン

同　マウチエ　チエレボヒン

同　アレキセイ　ウリヤノフ

同　ステハン　マルテミヤノフ

同　フエドロ　ハラハルヂン

103　ムールによる獄中からの上申書　上下

同　　　マタロス　　　　　　　ワシレエ　　　　　サハロフ

カムチャッカにて乗り組んだ者

同　　　　　　　　　　　　　ナワシャン　　　　セニン

同　　　　　　　　　　　　　イワン　　　　　　スエヅノフ

同　　　　　　　　　　　　　イワン　　　　　　ギリコリエフ

同　　　　　　　　　　　　　ヒリブ　　　　　　ラロマノフ

同　　　　　　　　　　　　　セメン　　　　　　クラレフ

同　　　　　　　　　　　　　タラス　　　　　　ワシリエフ

同　　　　　　　　　　　　　ラリヨン　　　　　チモフエエフ

同　　　　　　　　　　　　　セリブ　　　　　　チモフエエフ

同　　　　　　　　　　　　　ニキタ　　　　　　フエドロフ

同　　　　　　　　　　　　　フワテイ　　　　　エクセイエフ

同　　　　　　　　　　　　　イリヤ　　　　　　スツピン

〔註記‥1809年、海上で死亡した〕

同　　　ヘリヒウ　　　　　　キリコフ

同　　　セメン　　　　　　　コロツカイ

同　　　　チミイテレ

アメリカにて乗り組んだ者

マタロス　　　　　　　　　　イワン　　　シヤマエフ

同　　　　　　　　　　　　　ワシレエ　　ワシリエフ

同　　　　　　　　　　　　　タニロ　　　ボボフ

同　　　　　　　　　　　　　セルケー　　アウレツ

以上の通り乗り組んでいるとのことです。

　以上、ロシア人ムールが考え書き上げた文書をなるべく本文にある言葉を使い翻訳しました
が、その文章は、ほとんどが簡素で古色を帯びていましたので、やむを得ずところどころ文字
を補ったところがございます。かつまた文字を補っても意味が通じないところは、ムールに問
い合わせ、朱文で注解し差し上げた次第です。
　本文のうちにところどころ墨書にて註記したものも、本文にはなく、全く朱文同様にムール
本人に問い合わせたものでございます。
　本文人名など書き落としたところもありましたので、これも朱文注記として書き加えました。
ことばを話す速さが、日本語とは異なり格別に早いので、さまざまに展開すると、日本語に

ならないところもございます。はなはだしきに至っては、首尾が逆転し、しばらくして日本語の翻訳にかなうようなところもありましたので、翻訳はそのようにしましたところもございます。もっともこれまたなるべく本文の通り、前後の関係を考えて翻訳しましたので、かえって熟語にできず、文意も分からないような部分もあるように存じ奉ります。以上、全編、かなり翻訳いたしましたが、もとよりロシア言語・文字に不案内でございますので、ムールからいろいろ教授を受け翻訳しました。文意齟齬の部分も多くあろうかと存じますが、翻訳してみました。同人へも書いて読み聞かせ、問い合わせてみましたが、だいたいあっているように言っておりました。そうしたうえで書き上げ差し上げる次第です。以上

申〔岩下註：1812年、文化9年〕5月

村上貞助

あとがき

ムールの獄中上申書（「模烏児獄中上表」以下、本書）に出会ったのはいつであっただろうか。

最初に「明海大学図書館所蔵 『模烏児獄中上表』上下について（上）」を教え子にして畏友である松本英治氏と共著で『明海大学教養論文集』第11巻に発表したのは1999年12月だったから、かれこれ15年以上も前になる。

同論文を見ると、本書は1998年に明海大学図書館が購入したとあるから、16年以上ということになるだろう。当時、図書館で本書を手に取った時、これは大事な文献だと直感したことはよく覚えている。早速写真に撮影し、松本氏と手分けして解読し釈文を作成した。その文中にナポレオンの記述があることが大いに気になっていた。

もともと学部の卒業論文で江戸時代におけるナポレオンの受容史を研究し、1993年には卒論をもとにした論文「開国前後の日本における西洋英雄伝とその受容」を『洋学史研究』10号に発表していた。さらにそのころはちょうど、1999年に刊行した『江戸のナポレオン伝説』（中公新書）の刊行準備の真っ最中だったからだ。残念ながら中公新書には本書の内容は反映できなかったが、その後、「明海大学図書館所蔵 『模烏児獄中上表』上下について（上）」の続きである「同（中）」、「同（下・完）」を『明海大学教養論文集』第12巻（2000年）、『同』

第15巻（2003年）に松本氏とともに発表した。それゆえ、2006年の『江戸の海外情報ネットワーク』（吉川弘文館歴史文化ライブラリー）や2009年の「江戸時代における日露関係史上の主要事件に関する史料について」（竹内誠監修『外国人が見た近世日本』角川学芸出版）、2011年の「一八世紀～一九世紀初頭における露・英の接近と近世日本の変容」（笠谷和比古編『一八世紀日本の文化状況と国際環境』思文閣出版）には、ムールの獄中上申書研究の成果を十分に取り込むことができたと思う。

そうしたなかで、私は2つの課題を持つようになった。1つはムール獄中上申書の全文を書籍として刊行したい、いやすべきだということだ。その際、重要なのは、まず原文に最も近い江戸時代日本語から現代日本語にして、さらに現代日本語から英語にして、未だムール獄中上申書の存在を十分に知らないロシアやヨーロッパやアメリカに紹介したいということである。

ムールの上司ゴローウニンは『日本幽囚記』を執筆し、ヨーロッパの日本学発展に大いに寄与したが、その陰に隠れてしまったムールの獄中上申書をぜひとも再認識してほしいと思ったのである。それは、まさに江戸時代後期に『日本幽囚記』のオランダ語版が長崎から入ってきて、江戸の天文方が翻訳を始めたとき、ムールの獄中上申書を参考にしたことから、その差異に気づき、ムールの獄中上申書の写本を蒐集して底本を作成し、オランダ語訳してアムステルダムで刊行しようとしたことを約200年後に実現することでもあった。今回、最良の共編者アン

108

ナ・カーランデル　リネアさん（スウェーデン国籍）と知り合い、これが実現できたことは大変うれしいことである。つまり、1813年、銃で自殺したムールの無念を201年ぶりに晴らし、シーボルト事件（1828年）で弾圧された天文方の思いを186年ぶりに顕彰することができたのである。

アンナさんとの出会いは、突然だったが、随所で必然を感じた。それは2014年の2月28日金曜日昼、椿山荘で行われた小石川ロータリークラブの会合であった。この会にお導きくださったのは雄松堂書店会長新田満夫氏だった。新田氏に依頼されて私が「ペリー来航秘話」を講演した時、米山奨学金給付生として早稲田大学4年生のアンナさんも同会に出席し、会食のとき、同じテーブルでことばを交わした。その際、アンナさんが最初、明海大学外国語学部に入学して、その後、早稲田大学に移籍したこと、卒論のテーマで翻訳関係をやりたいと言っていたことを聞いた。その後、何度かのメールのやりとりから、ムールの獄中上申書の話になり、ロシア語も堪能なアンナさんが関心を示され、実際に明海大学図書館で「模烏児獄中上表」を見てもらい、私が作成するムール獄中上申書の現代日本語を英語に翻訳する過程から生じる問題などを卒論のテーマにすることに決められた。

それからが、実は大変だった。私は忙しい勤務の中、毎日余暇を見つけては、少しずつ現代語訳した。しかし、ロシア語から翻訳した江戸時代日本語の解釈ほど難しいものはない。ロシ

ア語原文があれば、原意が判明するが、今はそれはない。江戸時代日本語と乏しい19世紀西洋史等の知識で翻訳していった。それでも何とか、5月連休明けには作成し、アンナさんに御送りした。アンナさんも9月卒業に向けて相当頑張って英語に翻訳したと考えられる。その際、アンナさんのロシア語や欧州史の知識がかなり役立ったと推察する。7月から8月にかけて、都内のファミレス等で翻訳上の疑問点を解決する会合を何度持ったか分からない。こうして、無事アンナさんは卒論を出すことができた。審査はこれまた明海大学にも非常勤講師でいらっしゃった佐藤あずさ先生で、ここにも御縁を感じた。こうして出来上がった原稿を右文書院の三武義彦社長に見ていただき、出版のご快諾を得ることができ、青柳隆雄氏の編集により、今こうして公刊することができた。実に感無量である。この書物が多くの方々の目に留まることが出来たら幸いである。

そして2つの課題のうちのもう一つは、ペトロパブロフスク・カムチャッキーで自殺したムールのために、ゴローウニンが『日本幽囚記』のなかで立派な墓碑文が書かれた墓を建てたと書いているが、その現物を未だ誰も確認したことがないのである。これを現地で確認したいというのがもう一つの課題である。本来なら、本書巻頭口絵にその写真を載せたかった。だが、ペトロパブロフスク・カムチャッキーは遠く、直行便もなく、調査日数も調査費用（ガイド、車等）もかなりかかりそうで、（おそらくざっと見積もっても200万以上かかりそうで）、とて

も実現できなかった。

しかしながら、史上初、日本に帰化を希望したロシア人であり、日本に最初にナポレオン情報をもたらした人物であり、何よりも日本にシンパシーを持っていながら、30そこそこで亡くなったロシアの若者である。彼の、上申書以外で唯一と言ってもよい、この世に生きた証（墓）をぜひ見つけたいと思う。できるだけ、近いうちに訪問したい。

こうした思いを述べて筆を擱く。

2016年　岩下哲典

付記

先の「あとがき」は2016年に刊行を予定して準備したものである。しかしながら、2016年4月に私自身の職場が、明海大学から東洋大学かわって超多忙になって刊行を準備する時間がとれなくなってしまった。加えて、同時期、アンナさんが、早稲田大学をムールの卒論を書かれて無事に卒業され、帰国・就職された。それにより、お互いにメルアドを喪失し、しばらく音信不通になってしまった。

さらに右文書院三武義彦社長が、体調を崩され、事業を整理されたことなど、いくつかのやむを得ない事情が重なり、本書刊行の話しが一時立ち消えになっていた。

その後、元気になられた三武社長からご連絡をいただき、また、アンナさんのフェイスブックを見つけて連絡を取ることができ、刊行の準備が再開できたのが、コロナ禍の2020年9月であった。

こうしてなんとか、刊行準備の再開に漕ぎつけることができ、本当にうれしく思う。三武社長に感謝申し上げる。しかしながら、本書の刊行を楽しみにされ、いろいろと支援を惜しまなかった、雄松堂書店の会長であられた新田満夫氏がすでに亡くなってしまわれたことは、痛恨の極みである。心からご冥福をお祈りしたい。

112

また、今回は、翻訳家・古文書研究者イアン・アーシーさんには、アンナさんとネット上で再開するために、なにかとご助言をいただいた。記してお礼申し上げたい。

そして時間がたっていることから、もう一度、再点検をされたいと申し出ていただき、短い時間で目を通されたアンナさんに心からお礼申し上げる。

末筆ながら、本書刊行までには多くの方々の協力をいただいた。特に松本英治さん、濱口裕介さん、横田安正さん・横田リサさん父娘にはたいへんご尽力いただいた。記してお礼申し上げたい。

本書刊行が、日露関係史の新たな史料提供になり、ムールの心を210年ぶりに慰めることになれば幸いである。

2020年9月25日　岩下哲典

Imprisoned by the Edo Shogunate.

Moor's Agony

The True Story of the Russian Naval Lieutenant
from the Golovnin Incident.

Author of original:
Fedor Fedorvich Moor, Russian Naval Officer

Co-editor:
Tetsunori Iwashita, Professor at Toyo University
&
Anna Linnea Carlander, Translator

Publisher:
Yubunshyoin
1-5-6 Kandasurugadai Chiyodaku Tokyo
2021

CONTENTS

Dedicated to the memory of F. F. Moor and Teisuke Murakami

Explanatory Notes

1.　This document constitutes the prison report written by the Russian naval officer Fedor Fedorvich Moor, who came to Japan's Kunashiri Island at the beginning of the 19th century and was subsequently arrested and imprisoned by the Japanese. Among those imprisoned was also Vasilij Mihailovich Golovnin. After returning home to Russia, Golovnin authored and published his *Narrative of my Captivity in Japan during the Years 1811, 1812 & 1813*, but Moor's report remained unpublished.

2.　The whereabouts of the original report written in Russian by Moor are as yet unknown.

3.　Copies of the Russian original written in Edo period Japanese and translated by the Japanese interpreter Teisuke Murakami can today be found at Hokkaido University, the Hakodate Municipal Library, Meikai University, Waseda University, the National Archives, the National Diet Library, Nagoya's Hōsa Library, and the International Research Center for Japanese Studies, to name some places.

4.　Among these, the copy of *Moor's Report from Prison* (1 book) that belongs to the Meikai University Media Center (Library) is of comparatively good quality. It will from here on be referred to as "the Meikai copy."

5.　In the making of this book, Testunori Iwashita transcribed the original Meikai copy's contents into modern Japanese characters. He then translated this into present-day Japanese, which Anna Carlander then translated into present-day English while consulting the original Japanese.

6.　The Explanatory Notes, Commentary, and Conclusion was also writ-

ten by Iwashita in Japanese and translated into English by Carlander.

7.   This work thus consists of the following sections: Explanatory Notes (in present-day Japanese and English); a Commentary (present-day Japanese and English); the text of the Report itself (Edo period Japanese, present-day Japanese, and present-day English); and a Conclusion (present-day Japanese and English).

8.   The "Translator's notes" found in the Japanese text were written by Murakami Teisuke, who translated the original text from Russian into Japanese.

A commentary on "The Report from Prison Written by the Russian Officer Moor During His Confinement in Early 19th Century Japan" & Japanese Intelligence on Napoleon in the 19th Century

Introduction

The following introduction aims to provide a commentary on "The Report from Prison Written by the Russian Officer Moor During His Confinement in Early 19th Century Japan," and to discuss in detail the Golovnin incident's relation to intelligence regarding Napoleon Bonaparte. But before proceeding further, let us observe how foreign intelligence was administrated under the Edo Period Tokugawa Bakufu.

The foreign relations of the Tokugawa Bakufu during the mid-17th to 19th century – i.e. the time before ports and trade were opened up – are often described using the expression *sakoku*, or "closed country." However, this term came into being as late as during the 19th century, when the Japanese translated and coined it from the work of a former visitor to Japan, the German Engelbert Kaempfer. The meaning of the term also poses a problem since the reality of the situation was far more complex than it would indicate.

That the main object of foreign relations in modern Japanese history – and the greatest interest of its statesmen – was to ban of Christianity (1612) goes without saying; the religion threatened to undermine the current system. To prevent an influx of Christian teachings, the arrival of people, wares

and information from abroad had to be controlled and managed. The following policies were adopted in rapid succession for this specific purpose.

A Nagasaki magistrate was established and Nagasaki was put under the direct governance of the Bakufu (1633). Japanese were moreover forbidden to travel outside of the country's borders (1635), and Portuguese ships were banned (1639). The Dutch were confined to Dejima (1641) and the Bakufu's trading activities were limited to Nagasaki, with trade only being conducted with China and Holland. A system heavily reliant on Holland and China for foreign intelligence thus came to develop (besides these two countries, information was also gathered from shipwrecked foreigners and castaways who had managed to make their way home again).

The defense of the port of Nagasaki was the responsibility of the Fukuoka, Saga and Ōmura clans, and were part of their military service. Trade with the Ainu was meanwhile made the responsibility of the Matsumae clan by the Bakufu (1604), and relations with the Kingdom of Korea fell to the Tsushima clan (1607-). Relations with the Kingdom of Ryukyu were the Satsuma clan's responsibility (1609, 1634-). A nationwide coastal defense system and intelligence network was further installed during the Kan'ei era, and the Dutch were made to write regular reports on current events in the world as proof of their goodwill (1644-, made part of the system officially in 1659). The reality of the so-called sakoku policy came to develop in this manner. However, due to the success of research on China's Kaikin policy (which forbade private individuals to trade with foreign countries) it has in recent years also come to be referred to as kaikin. But this term too is a

modern one and so is not originally designed to fit the actual circumstances of Japan's international relations from Iemitsu onwards. It is my opinion that "sakoku" is thus a less appropriate term used mostly for expediency's sake when discussing foreign relations in modern Japan.

1. The Golovnin Incident and *Moor's Report from Prison*

As previously noted, the foreign relations of the Tokugawa Bakufu – i.e. sakoku policy – were restricted to "corresponding countries" like the Ryukyu and Korea, with whom the Bakufu exchanged diplomatic letters and envoys, and "trading countries" such as China (the Ming and Qing dynasties) and Holland. But then in the latter half of the 16th century, Russia began its advance into the Far East and in the mid eighteen hundreds a Russian warship under the command of Schpanberg Martin Petrovich (his Russian name; Schpanberg's Danish name was Morten Spangberg) appears off the coast of Japan. Towards the end of the century, an envoy from Russia – Laxman – visits Nemuro to request that Japan's ports and cities be opened for trade. The Russian Rezanov is similarly met with rejection by the Bakufu during his visit to Nagasaki at the beginning of the 19th century, and the Tokugawa Bakufu strengthens its guard against the North when Rezanov's subordinates later attack Yezo as if in retaliation for their refusal. The island of Yezo, to all intents and purposes under the direct control of the Bakufu, was in other words on high alert against an attack by Russia.

Not knowing of this, Captain Golovnin of the Russian naval sloop the Diana approaches Japan in 1811, having received an order to survey the North Pacific. Upon going ashore at Kunashiri Island with a handful of

men, he and his companions are arrested by the Bakufu and imprisoned in Matsumae. The vice-captain still left aboard the Diana, Petr Rikord, kidnaps a government patronized merchant in retaliation, Takadaya Kahei. An exchange of prisoners is later agreed upon and in 1813, the incident reaches its conclusion. The events leave the Bakufu with a positive impression of Russians as good, honest neighbors. Regrettably, few Japanese share that view today.

Among the men imprisoned together with Golovnin, there was a Russian soldier called Lieutenant Moor. As Golovnin and the others plan their escape in 1812, the year following their arrest, Moor alone declines to join them. With his talent for drawing Moor had quickly found a way to communicate with the Japanese through pictures, and he begins to long for naturalization in Japan, wishing to work for its government (the Bakufu) as a translator of Western languages. One may recognize in Moor the very beginnings of the state referred to as "Cultural Translation" by Dr. Youichi Nagashima. According to Nagashima, "cultural translation" is the ability to "observe the world through 'another's' eyes, juxtapose one's own cultural background to that of the other individual, and possess the bicultural [a state of belonging to two cultures or immersing oneself in two cultures] ability to have a holistic view of the whole of both cultures." While it is unclear whether Moor reached a point where he had a holistic view of both Japan's and Russia's cultures, he did at the very least feel appreciation for Japan. However to be naturalized in Japan and work as an interpreter of foreign languages (mainly Western ones), he had to have compared Russia to Japan and considered abandoning the former state, something that does indicate that he saw his

own mother country in a relative manner. The phenomenon of cultural translation had no doubt begun to manifest in him.

But be that as it may, Moor did not copy the actions of Golovnin and escape. Moor is indubitably the first Russian in history to long for naturalization in Japan and thus he deserves special mention. Incidentally, it was also the still imprisoned Moor who later produced the document which came to be called *Moor's Report from Prison* (*Muuru gokujū jyōhyō*), a work significant not only to the history of Russo-Japanese relations but also the entire history of foreign relations in Japan. The Report, written in in Russian, was translated into Japanese by the translator Teisuke Murakami and then presented to the Bakufu's Council of Elders via the Matsumae magistrate's office.

The Report contains Moor's account of the following: the feelings that prompted him to write the document; Rezanov's visit to Nagasaki; Golovnin's duties and history; Rezanov's subordinate Khvostov's attack on Yezo; Golovnin's escape; the state of affairs in Russia and Europe, and finally, Napoleon. This was at the time all highly significant information to the Bakufu, but I will limit myself to discussing the intelligence given on Napoleon, as it held particular value for modern Japan.

Moor's Report from Prison is the earliest ever written record of Napoleon. Until now it was believed that an article on Napoleon in a Russian newspaper brought to Japan in 1813 was the earliest source, but we now know that the oldest known intelligence is this report dating from 1812. It

was in other words the Dutch merchant office's persistent efforts to keep Napoleon's existence a secret that resulted in the information entering Japan not through Nagasaki in the south, but Yezo in the north – and then via a group of Russians who only happened to be arrested there. In the previously mentioned Russian newspaper, brought to Japan by Captain Rikord, it was stated that the former capital of Holland, Amsterdam, had been made the Third City of the Napoleon Empire by Napoleon's imperial decree. The truth of this matter was confirmed with the Dutch merchant's office in Nagasaki and, Dejima. The Dutch in Nagasaki then mustered the excuse that, "such a report has not yet been received but it is quite possible that it is so." But even having been told this, the Bakufu had no means to verify the validity of the statement. There was a limit to what could be done with only one source of information on the West.

2. The Bakufu Tenmonkata's plans to publish *Moor's Report from Prison* in Europe

It is also worth noting that the Bakufu's top-level research organ on Western learning, science and information, the Tenmonkata – originally an organization for the production of calendars and maps – was laying plans for new developments in foreign relations not long after this.

In 1816, Golovnin publishes his *Narrative of my Captivity in Japan 1811-1813* in Russia. The work makes its way to Nagasaki via Holland and is from there presented to the Tenmonkata. In 1825, having promptly translated the Dutch copy, they discover that the work differs from *Moor's Report from Prison* on a number of points. While Moor had written his report

with feelings of affection for Japan, Golovnin appears not to have shared his sentiments. Those Tenmonkata who had read Moor's version first no doubt found Golovnin's work inconsistent with the truth. They thus began collecting copies of *Moor's Report from Prison*, from which they created a standardized edition. They translated this into Dutch, and requesting the assistance of the merchant's office and Dutch individuals alike, they made plans to publish the work in Amsterdam and throughout Europe. Their intention was to have the people of Europe judge who was correct – Golovnin or Moor. And had not the advocate of this plan, Shomotsu Bugga (Magistrate of Books), and Tenmonkata Kageyasu Takahashi, lost his position due to the Siebold Incident in 1828, it might indeed have been realized. One of the reasons Takahashi backed Siebold to such an extent may have been because of his wish to carry out this Amsterdam publication plan. Takahashi's greatest expectation was naturally to gather information regarding the current state of affairs in Europe, but one can surmise that he also intended to send out intelligence about Japan in Europe. If this was the case then this could indeed be called a high-level intelligence gathering effort on the part of one section of the Bakufu body: an unprecedented plan to not only gather but also broadcast intelligence, thereby changing public opinion in Europe. That such a plan could be drawn up by an Edo period man is something to take pride in.

However, these ideas were not unique to the Tenmonkata – Japan's *rangaku* (Western studies) scholars were also thinking in similar ways. It is for instance believed that the 1774 translation of the Kaitai Shinsho (*Anatomische Tabellen*) was written in *kanbun* (classical Chinese) since it was as-

sumed it would be read not only in Japan but in all the regions using Chinese characters, especially in China. This is said to be the reason that you even today find words in Chinese medical terminology that entered the language via Japan.

The Bakufu medical officer Hoken Katsuragawa was furthermore recommended as a member of the oldest international society in the East, the Batavian Society of Arts and Sciences. With the occurrence of such events, the so-called sakoku policy became irreconcilable with the wishes of the Tenmonkata and rangaku scholars. In short, the more one worried for the future of Japan, the more the sakoku policy that obstructed further intelligence gathering efforts turned into nothing more than fetters. And as long as that did not change, intelligence gathering could not be anything but a covert activity. Still, in some cases the rangaku scholars' activities were discovered anyway and criticized by the Bakufu as stirring up trouble. The Siebold Incident in 1828 and the *"bansha no goku"* (the indictment of the society for Western study) in 1839 are two striking examples of this. The incidents appear to have strangled the efforts of rangaku scholars.

3. Intelligence regarding Napoleon following the Golovnin Incident

Incidentally, the Tenmonkata Kageyasu Takahashi had also inferred that conditions in Europe had changed by observing the changes in the appearance of the clothing that the head of the Dutch merchant's office wore when he made his customary visits to Edo. The result of these observations became the 1826 *Heijutsu Ibun* (『丙戌異聞』) and *Berearianse Senki* (『別埒阿

利安設戦記』). The former is a simple biography about Napoleon and the latter a record of war focusing on the battle of Waterloo. But as Kageyasu passed away in prison after the Siebold Incident, his research was succeeded by Sanei Koseki, a medical officer of the Kishiwada clan and newly appointed Bakufu Tenmonkata as well as employee of the Bakufu's translation agency.

Sanei takes over Kageyasu's work with a critical eye and translates the short biography *Bonaparte Ryakuden* (『卜那把盧的略伝』) (circa 1829) as well as the *Napoleon-den* (『那波列翁伝』) from 1832 up to his suicide during the Bansha no goku – the "Indictment of the society for western (or barbarian) study" – in 1839. The latter publication ends with the Treaty of Amiens and is thus only half-finished as a biography over the life of Napoleon, but it does contain references to the Revolution and is the most detailed of the Edo period Napoleon biographies. Later on men like the Hamamatsu clan doctor Bokuchū Maki and the Tsuyama clan doctor Genpo Mitsukuri draw inspiration from the work and make it their goal to complete an even more substantial biography. In 1857, the Tahara clan officer Yoken Matsuoka publishes the biographies Sanei produced, and consequently the Matsushiro clan scholar Shōzan Sakuma and Chōshū officer Shōin Yoshida later produce classical Chinese poems, and Satsuma officer Takamori Saigō superimposes Napoleon on himself – the works come have a significant influence on the great men of the Bakumatsu era.

Besides these examples, a chief retainer of the Koga clan, Senseki Takami, collects various goods related to Napoleon from Holland: copperplate

3. Intelligence regarding Napoleon following the Golovnin Incident (11)

prints of the battle of Italy; soldier figures made out of lead, and Lord Nelson commemorative accessory cases. He also produces detailed maps of the country of Holland, and this too can surely be said to be due to the impact of Napoleon intelligence. Senseki also makes a reference to the arrival of Russian ships in his 1853 opinion paper, written during Perry's arrival in Japan. He writes that, "In September that same year, 'Golovnin,' 'Moor' and the others returned on the boat sent to retrieve them." That such a comment is to be found among Senseki's writings is noteworthy as it suggests that *Moor's Report from Prison* played a part in his education on foreign matters. And there is indeed a copy of *Moor's Report from Prison* among the Takami family's collection of documents found at the Koga Museum of History. It is no doubt an old possession of Senseki's.

At the very end of the Bakumatsu period, in 1867, Genichirō Fukuchi writes the *Napoleon Heihou* (『那破倫兵法』), perhaps in preparation for the coming Boshin War.

In 1867, the last Shogun, Yoshinobu Tokugawa, submits the so-called "Restoration of Imperial Rule" petition (a petition to restore political power, to be exact) to the Imperial Court. At this point he is still only saying that political power will be returned to the Emperor – he has yet to do so in reality. What Yoshinobu hoped for was a Napoleon-style Empire, and for himself to occupy the seat of Napoleon. But as the Restoration of Imperial Rule and Imperial Administration became an inevitability, his designs fell through and the one who came to occupy Napoleon's position was the Meiji Emperor.

Yet the Bakufu army's French military advisors, among them Jules Brunet, still fought alongside Takeaki Enomoto and others in various battles, going as far up north as Hakodate. Brunet even directed the construction of the fort Shiryōkaku. The French officer sympathized with the pro-French group in the old Bakufu military. And surprisingly enough, the Meiji government awarded Brunet with a medal in 1882 as well as in 1895; pro-French Japanese were to be found also in the Meiji government. This indicates just how widely read Napoleon's biographies were among Japanese at the time, regardless of whether they belonged to the Bakufu or Meiji government – intelligence on Napoleon was the evidence and witness sought by the thinkers of late modernity, end-of-Bakumatsu Restoration years, and Meiji period alike. Napoleon died on Saint Helena in 1821, but both in the Boshin War forty-seven years later and in the Sino-Japanese War seventy years on, he lived on unforgotten in the hearts of the Japanese.

Conclusion

This concludes the discussion of the role and importance of intelligence on Napoleon in Japan during the latter half of the Edo period and Bakumatsu era. First we noted that the earliest intelligence to be brought into Japan appeared right in the middle of the Golovnin Incident at the beginning of the 19th century, and consisted of a report from prison written by the Russian soldier Moor, a member of the Golovnin party. The impact this information had on the then highest research organ on Western affairs, the Tenmonkata, was significant. We further discussed the Tenmonkata's attempt to publish this prison report in Amsterdam and Europe with the help of the Dutch

merchant's office and other Dutch individuals, as well as the results of their plan. We also mentioned that the Tenmonkata was later forced to restrict their activities due to political pressure from the Bakufu authorities, and that research on Napoleon was continued by one rangaku scholar, Sanei Koseki, whose works later influenced such men as Shōzan Sakuma, Shōin Yoshida and Takamori Saigō. Senseki Takami and Yoshinobu Tokugawa's relationship to Napoleon was also discussed. The way in which information about Napoleon impacted late Edo period and Bakumatsu-era Japan was thus summarized. And lastly, the pro-French faction in the inner circles of the Bakufu and Meiji government and the French military advisers were also mentioned.

To conclude this introduction, the Golovnin Incident and *Moor's Report from Prison* was nothing less than crucial to the communication and spread of information on Napoleon. It is indeed a remarkable case deserving of special mention as it happened not only at the absolute earliest point in which our country could have gained access to such intelligence, but also in how the information came not from Nagasaki, the city traditionally thought of as important to foreign intelligence gathering, but the north, and lastly, because of the Bakufu's intelligence organization's plans to publish this report in foreign land.

Moor's Prison Report

The following is a translation of a letter written in Western letters by the Russian national Moor.

A record of the Author's thoughts.

To the Emperor[1] of the Great Empire[2] of Japan's magistrates of the local garrison towns Matsumae, Kunashiri, Etorofu[3] and others, Ogasawara Ise-no-kami and Arao Tanba-no-kami.

With humble regards, His Imperial Majesty of Russia's naval officer, Moor.

1.

The magistrate's office has shown us great consideration and kindness during the past year. Not a day or night have passed when we have not thought that should the chance to appear before the Emperor someday arrive, we would like to tell of all the kindness we have received. As we offer

---

[1] Iwashita: The title of the head of the *Bakufu* government (征夷大将軍).

[2] Carlander: The original letter calls Japan *"dainippon teikoku"* (大日本帝国), a name which came into common use during the Meiji Period. It is most often translated as "the Empire of Greater Japan," but has come to be strongly associated with Japan's colonialist policy during the latter half of the Meiji Period and first half of the 20th century. To avoid any confusion with this politically charged name and to stay true to the respectful tone that Moor surely wished to convey, the translation henceforth used shall be "the Great Empire of Japan."

[3] Carlander: In his *Narrative of my captivity in Japan*, Captain Golovnin called Matsumae *"Matsmai"* and Kunashiri *"Kunaschier."* Etorofu is the Japanese name of Iturup.

up our heartfelt prayers for the health of all of the officials, we hope to remember this time for a long time to come.

When my companions recently yielded their hearts to evil temptation and escaped, disregarding the gracious kindness shown to us, I and the other Russian who had met with disaster[4] were once more thrown into darkness. We believed that all previously shown cordiality would be lost to us. However, at the magistrate's office they showed great mercy, sympathizing with the feelings of those who had escaped and giving no blame but only an even more compassionate admonition. Now that the thought of returning home has come to be associated with despair, it weighs heavy on my mind to not be able to repay the kindness shown to us. Moreover, for every day that passes, my concepts of chivalry and faith change and I can feel my intellect gradually grow poorer. How should I spend the time given me? Wishing to repay even just a fraction of the kindness shown to us by the magistrate's office, I would like to record all that is in my heart herein.

2.

By Russian law we are strictly forbidden to do anything that might cause foreigners to loathe Russia or otherwise bring shame upon her. In addition to this, this country is in its customs quite suspicious of foreign nations, something that is hard to understand not only for us but also for navigators from European states. According to what a Japanese told me, there is even a saying here: "To sail seas full of reefs and sandbars is to voluntarily invite

---

[4] Carlander: The Kurile Alexei.

disaster." Such things have made me keep quiet until now.

3.

We had never set foot on Japanese soil before this. It was not until we went ashore on Etorofu Island that we learned that it belonged to Japan. However, none in our company mentioned this when we were admitted into the officials' presence, likely reassuring them. Though we received numerous instructions and letters before our departure, we gradually grew short on provisions. Striving to follow our teachings in the various unavoidable situations that resulted, we kept quiet about some things in an effort to avoid deceit. But while those with a dishonorable character seem to always have a scheme for every situation, those who are pure of heart will project their own values onto them and believe them to be as innocent of malicious intent as they are. The present troubles are a consequence of this.

During our questioning in Hakodate, we were asked if we had come to Japan to steal or to wage war, but there were good reasons for both questions. Until that point we had not known what had been clearly communicated to Erezanov [Translator's note: This Erezanov is the same Rezanov who came to Nagasaki. When translating the letters this time they were transcribed as "Erezanov," and so I left it thus.][5], that, "Should a Russian ship come to Japan hereafter, it will be destroyed by fire." When we heard of this, we felt as if struck by lightning, and we despaired of ever being able

---

[5] Carlander: Nikolai Petrovich Rezanov (1764-1807), Russian ambassador to Japan in 1804. Called "Resanoff" in Golovnin's *Narrative*.

to return home. We were further told of Khvostov's[6] attacks and questioned minutely, but needless to say these were the actions of another and therefore not something I know much about. Neither do I know what evidence to base my statements on or if I should go into detail, for while I know some things about this matter, I do not know enough to speak of it in detail.

To summarize, we set sail from Russia on the instructions of a Russian mainland official, Isprawnik [official title] Romakin [name]. We were to observe the island of Yezo[7] since lately foreigners from the Kurile Islands had come to Etorofu more frequently in pursuit of personal gain. Four ships were sent to Matsumae and three to *Mohanai*. [Translator's note: *Mohanai* seems to be how the Russians call the area stretching from the three islands of Etorofu, Kunashiri and Shikotan to Matsumae. It is said the name comes from the full beards of the natives.] We had no intention whatsoever to do battle, and telling lies is something we learned how to do only after being imprisoned. From what I had been told while still onboard, we had only been sent to do trade. It is the fault of such lies coming from all directions that we now find ourselves in such difficulties. Furthermore, just as we had been told since long ago, the manner of the Japanese we met was deeply suspicious. We were at a loss as to how to explain ourselves. For above reasons I have been unable to share many things until now.

---

[6] Carlander: Nicholas Alexander Khvostov.
[7] Iwashita: Hokkaido.

[Translator's note: The foreigners from the Kurile Islands mentioned herein refer to the Rashowans who came to Etorofu two years earlier, and the lie that they had told, denying that a number of Russian ships had come to Matsumae and Etorofu. Alexei apparently first revealed this to Moor while they were incarcerated in the Hakodate prison. According to what he said at that time, they had all to a man told this lie, afraid that if they were to reveal the truth, the Japanese officials would think it was the fault of one shrewd individual and the rest would be ordered to return to their country while only one of them was detained. Though reluctant, they therefore continued to tell the story their companion had first come up with. Alexei confided this to Moor, who considered the matter and came to the conclusion that even if it were a lie, should Alexei tell the truth now it would please the Japanese officials. This coincides with what the Rashowans stated during their reexamination in Kunashiri, as well as with the statements of the commanding official there.]

4.

Not long ago, I was commanded by the grace of the magistrate's office to record the sequence of events which led to our arrival in Japan. I thereafter submitted an application and report, wherein I may have omitted certain things, but told no lies. I stand by my statements even now. Even in the event that a Russian official would hereafter read these documents, I believe they would agree, and be familiar enough with Japanese customs, to understand that the difficulties we have encountered were inevitable and in no way caused by malicious intent.

5.

I am grateful for the understanding the magistrate's office has shown us. In the detailed statement I have written on this occasion, I am prepared to repent the things I have done during my lifetime at the time of my death, and so I only wish for the magistrate's office to read it. I moreover wish to clear the suspicions held until now.

6.

Neither was there any evil intent behind my companions' attempt to escape on this occasion; thinking only of returning to their motherland, they had begun to perceive insults where no insult was intended and lost their senses, forgetting the merciful teachings of the magistrate's office. When they were captured and returned to the magistrate's office, they gave the illogical excuse that such an escape would have been permitted by Russian law, and the magistrate's office excused them saying that they must have lost their heads, but I cannot help but feel embarrassed. For while barbarians may lack a legislative system, and barbarian countries' laws may only be□□□, European countries' laws, though they slightly vary, are all based on the notion of man's integrity. I was therefore until now unaware that escaping would be considered acceptable behavior. I believe it was their confusion that made them say such a thing. I ask that you take pity on them.

7.

If one meets with robbery or a holdup, or is taken prisoner during battle, escape may be considered acceptable as long as you haven't given your

word of honor to the enemy general. But we do find it truly strange. We only came to Kunashiri out of great need, and even brought with us a letter from a Japanese official. Hence, we asked for aid, but were answered with bullets. [Translator's note: Having received a letter from Ishizaka Kihei, the Russians believed that they would be free to go anywhere in Japan. Thinking also that their wishes would be quickly understood with it, the captain set out for shore in a small boat the morning after ship's arrival, but it was met with such violent fire that he could not land. I am told it is this answer of bullets to their letter that made Moor phrase himself in this manner.] Having no other choice, we then took some older provisions for ourselves, but left copper plates and some modest gifts in return. Later when going ashore, these compensatory gifts were returned to us, but as we were about to refuse them we were arrested and treated like thieves. Though the inquiry is not yet over, I am grateful and glad for how the magistrate's office has pardoned us and treated us mercifully.

It hardly needs saying that according to the law one cannot plan to escape while under investigation, no matter what the reason. [Translator's note: It is not explicitly stated in Europe's laws that one cannot, regardless of reason, flee while still under investigation. Moor tells me he phrased himself thusly since he feels the time of inquiry should be spent in repentance, in particular all the more so if one is guilty, and that no matter what justification one may have, escaping before a sentence is passed would be to leave before things were properly resolved.] At a time when it is only the mercy of the magistrate's office that holds us together, escape is unthinkable. But even if we come to be punished as thieves by Japan's officials our

sins may still be forgiven, and so as an honorable man I have resolved to act in a manner that will not cause shame. Since ancient times it has happened that even high ranked officials and virtuous men have been imprisoned and ended their lives on the execution grounds. Therefore, if worse comes to worst and we are sentenced to death, it is not up to us to decide if our sins should be forgiven, but surely God or the Russian Emperor that will save us.

My companions' escape attempt – undertaken without any warning whatsoever after the arrival of spring this year, fooling both me and Alexei who disagreed with it – was something done out of a longing for home and while in a state of confusion, I believe. There is a Russian proverb that says, "a drowning man will cling to anything." They say that even if it is a knife that is held out he will still grasp for it, not caring if his fingers are cut off. My companions were truly in just such a situation as this proverb describes. The magistrate's office has shown a great understanding for this and spoken to us with vast mercy and pity, something we are deeply grateful for. In order not to further go against my sense of honor and shame, I therefore believe it is only proper to relay in detail all that is in my heart and mind and present it before the magistrate's office.

8.

Around the end of spring in the year 1806 [corresponding to the third year of Bunka in our calendar], the Russian state sloop Nadezhda [Name of a ship. Rezanov onboard. The ship that visited Nagasaki] and the American Company merchantman Neva [name of ship] set out on their first voyage around the world. The country rejoiced at their safe return, but they had

failed to fulfill one of the journey's objectives: an embassy to Japan. Nadezhda's captain, Krusenstern,[8] and the other officers onboard consulted with
each other about why the delegation had failed, arriving at the conclusion
that the foremost reason lay with Rezanov's impatient and proud personali-
ty which had manifested itself on several occasions, showing how unsuit-
able he was for the position of envoy. This, along with the distrustful manner of the Japanese, at times differing from that of Europeans, were seen as
the greatest reasons for why an alliance had not been achieved. Furthermore, because no one at that time thought to have an interpreter accompany
Rezanov, a Dutchman had had to interpret for him. The Japanese officials
and the Russians had trusted him, and it had not even occurred to them that
he might deceive them but it seems he did indeed. It was during the winter
of 1807 [sixth year of Bunka], when our sloop the Diana was at anchor in
British Portsmouth, that this was unexpectedly discovered.

I do not know this for sure, but considering the reply given to Rezanov
by the Japanese, it seems Japan's customs are quite different from Russia's
due to being located so far away. I am not very knowledgeable about European customs either so I do not know if this will be useful to Japan, but I
heard from an officer of the Nadezhda, Baron *Vilin*[9] [Translator's note: A
title corresponding to that of our country's daimyo or retainer, it seems.
Besides this one, there are other titles like *kniaz* and *graf.* They appear frequently hereafter: *kniaz, graf,* and *baron.* Most are barons, but since the

---

[8] Carlander: Adam Johann von Krusenstern.

[9] Carlander: Present-day Japanese translation reads as *bilin sawojin.* This may refer to Ensign
Baron Faddei Billingsgauzen, one of the crew on the Nadezhda.

original text is like this I have translated it thusly.] *Sawojin* [name] as well as other officers the general purport of what was communicated in Nagasaki: that further visits to Japan would not be allowed, and should a Japanese ship wash ashore on Russian shores, then Russian officials are to request the assistance of Holland, and the sailors to be escorted from Holland to Nagasaki by the Dutch. Unable to comprehend what purpose this could possibly serve, our countrymen decided not to dwell any further on Japan. Officials and merchants began to think of trading with other nations instead.

[Translator's note: The American Company mentioned herein is a merchant company which handles wares produced in the American provinces.]

The American provinces were not developed by any monarch but first colonized by merchants some time ago. Thus there are no officials stationed there. Some years back, merchants from the Okhotsk area sent out ships on their own initiative, traveling via the Aleutian Islands to the American provinces to trade and collect wares. But every year there were disputes and a number of people were injured or died. The greedy merchants often acted violently towards the natives. The wealthy Irkutsk merchant *Senbono*[10] then gathered together the merchants who travelled to the region every year and set up a company. With this the disputes came to an end, and since they acted to promote the education of the natives, the King and various officials gave their acknowledgement of the company. As a result, the company was

---

[10] Carlander: (センボノ) May be a corruption of the name of Grigorii Shelikhov (Shelekhov), one of the Russian-American Company's founders.

given the name "the American Company," office buildings were built, wealthy merchants got together to provide the capital, and the company came to handle American products. Neva is one of the company's ships.

One of the company members, Baranov,[11] had traveled to America ever since the company was founded. He built a stronghold in a place where there had long been a village called Kodiak, and then he went on to establish a village in a place called Yakutat. He stationed his vassals in both locations and had them guard the area. He then crossed over to an island called Sitka and built yet another village there, but setting fire to the previous settlements in Kodiak and Yakutat led to conflict with the natives. Thereafter he built new villages on both islands and merchants came to live there. Later, he had a great fortress built in a place called Novo-Arkhangelsk, and the merchant Baranov's home came to serve as the local government office. Ships from Russia came to anchor there as a rule.

By then Baranov had been given the official merchant title of Councilor of Commerce. The office corresponded to that of the chief official of the province. But this province was a distant frontier region and thus full of inconveniences, making him travel every year to Boston [Translator's note: also known as *Aleut-America*] or such to trade. Among the things he brought with him were guns, lead bullets, gunpowder and the like. In the places he traded with the natives he did not sell them weapons in case they were truly cruel barbarians, but neither did he hide them. Should they get their hands

---

[11] Carlander: Aleksandr Andreyevich Baranov (1746-1819).

on such wares, though, he would not be safe and so Baranov set up a new system. But making the laws known across all of the vast region was difficult, and so he discussed the issue with a company superintendent in the capital of Petersburg. He asked for a sloop per year to be sent to Novo-Arkhangelsk, so that even if people from Boston came they would not be able to trade these weapons. A chief official was also dispatched. When the mainland official traveled to Boston to discuss these matters, he was told by the officials of said location that if a boat carrying these wares turned up it would be acceptable to arrest the crew and punish them according to national laws. A chief official of the American provinces, *Bokovniki* [title] *Kouha* [name], passed away in Kamchatka after departing from Okhotsk. Our ship was thus ordered to set sail like the Neva.

[Translator's note: In the text, Moor expresses an inability to understand the intentions of the Japanese. This refers to how, despite Kamchatka being near Japan, they are not allowed to dispatch ships, forcing the Japanese who are washed ashore in this region to be sent from Holland to Batavia on Russia's request, and then from there on to Japan. The repatriation of the Japanese thus turns into a journey across land and sea spanning thousands of *ri.*[12] The result will be that many of those taken into protective custody will die halfway through after weakening from being dragged across freezing and equatorial regions. We too know well the distances of the earth, and this kind of thinking is unreasonable. I also believe that we are informed of changes in Europe by Holland from time to time. But it is not uncommon

---

[12] Carlander: One *ri* is approximately 3,9 km.

for alliances to change every year, and it is plausible that free travel through Europe would be impossible at times. We are well aware of this. With this in mind, being told something like the above makes it sound as if it does not matter whether the castaways are returned or not. Having learned of our country, and considering the benevolence that has reached even Yezo in the form of inviting and educating its people, this is unreasonable. Supposing that Emperor Alexander does not comprehend our intentions right now, even if requests to trade are made they might come to nothing. After all, Europe is a remote region and news are thus hard to relay; that cooperation among even neighboring is difficult is something even Russia knows well.]

9.

All nations are the same in how the actions of merchants differ from those of soldiers or peasants. Once, a North American ship that had traded in the Russian territory for many years sold some exceedingly poor wares, causing various troubles for those coming from Russia or navigating the high seas. The head of the local branch of the Company requested for those who tried to bring this kind of wares to be stopped at home. The merchants believed that if one state ship per year were to come to the American territory, the people from Boston would not dare try anything when they came. And so since the establishment of the Russian American Company, the Neva has been transporting goods to Novo-Arkhangelsk, where it takes on local products before heading to Canton to trade these before returning to Russia. Contemplating this at length, the chief officials of the Naval Department recalled that the transports shipping government goods held the same wares as the Neva, so why not send these to Okhotsk? And so we were ordered on

the request of the Company to transport goods to Okhotsk as well as guard the Neva as soon as the Diana had been finished. We were loaded with goods, provisions, and medical supplies and the like at the government office called the Admiralty Department. Captain Golovnin [Translator's note: This is the captain earlier referred to as "Gawabin". The name sounds like "Gawabin" when spoken, but is more accurately transcribed as "Golovin," which is why I have chosen to translate it thus.] was also given surveying instruments, books, maps and a copy of a naval chart guide called *Instorkcha* by the Military Department. The written orders Golovnin received from *Kenjara Majoro* [title] *Gamanja* [name] at this time said that there would be many countries and islands along the route he would sail, and though numerous navigators had surveyed them closely before he was to take this opportunity to investigate closely so that nothing had been omitted. Furthermore, there were still unknown areas in Okhotsk and the Kurile Islands, and so while en route to Okhotsk he was to take the time to record what he saw, as well as purchase the latest world atlas and guide on sea routes in Britain.

By the end of October [The end of October in the year 1806. Between the ninth and tenth month according to our calendar.], the Neva had been loaded with goods as well, but since the copper roofing on the Diana was still not finished she was delayed and the Neva set sail alone. After this various orders were given, and in the winter of 1806 [Referring to the months of December, January, and February in Russia. They correspond to the eleventh, twelfth and first month of our calendar. "Winter" will hereafter refer to this definition.] we were finally ordered by a chief official of the Naval Department called the *Minister of Moscoi* [title] *Hauvewashreuch*

Chichakov [name] to ship goods to the Kamchatka region again as soon as the Diana had been furnished.

10.

By the end of July year 1807 [Corresponding to the fourth year of Bunka in our calendar.], the Diana had been fully furnished and an order from the King been given to her officers, sailors and crew. It said to take her goods to Kamchatka, sail to America to join the Neva, and to stay on our guard while next sailing for the port of Canton. Both ships were to return to Petersburg as soon as the Neva had finished trading. I have written down the names of the crew this time separately herein. On this occasion, the King Himself inspected the Diana along with the Cronstadt fortress and some state ships on His way back from Prussia.

11.

On July 25, 1807, [End of the third month in Bunka year four according to our calendar.] the Diana had left Cronstadt and arrived in Pomerania. We could hear the tremendous sound of cannons firing. From there we sailed to a place called Copenhagen in Denmark, and just outside of the city we encountered a British ship which inquired about our nationality and destination. Captain Golovnin answered that we were a state ship sent to transport goods to Kamchatka. After this we gradually approached the city from the right side, entered port, and after showing our flag a pilot was sent to us. We again saw a tremendous number of British ships. The pilot told us, "It seems the British ships have surrounded the capital like this because they heard a Danish state ship was to be sent to Britain. The Danish officials are object-

ing and have begun preparing for battle." It seems there were some skirmishes involving firearms that night. A British warship also passed by the Diana during the night, but the cannon fire from the castle was so intense it was utterly destroyed. The ships that had escaped complete destruction passed by the Diana again as they retreated. The next day we met with an official of said location, Commodore [title] *Dowoken* [name] and a chief local official called *Heiner* [name], but both of them told us that, "As you can see, we are at present in the middle of battle, and so you cannot stay here. We would like for you to sail to Danish Elsinore instead." Thus we hurriedly set sail from Copenhagen. That night we stayed out on the open sea, and already the next morning the battle began.

Some time thereafter we reached Elsinore and replenished our provisions and water supply. Two days later, we set sail for Britain. We met with gales and saw numerous naval vessels from different countries. Upon reaching a place called Calais [an isthmus located on the border of France and Britain] we encountered a British ship and were asked many questions, so Captain Golovnin gave the same answers as he had in Denmark.

Forty days had passed in this manner since our departure from Cronstadt when we arrived at the British port of Portsmouth. The rumor there had it that Britain intended to go to war with Russia in the near future. We also spoke to Captain *Hourin* of the Russian government ship Siberia which had put in at the port before us. Golovnin then traveled to the British capital, London, to procure onboard necessities. In accordance with our orders from home he also went to receive receipts of bills of exchange from Canton, the

Cape of Good Hope and Brazilia, and to confer with merchants. While in London he also met a Russian official stationed there called *Baran Arabeus* and asked him for advice on what to do if a war between Britain and Russia broke out, and voyage on the Diana became difficult. He received the reply that since the other was unfamiliar with maritime problems and could not do anything about offshore matters, he had no answer. Golovnin also spoke with another Russian official stationed in London called *Volonia* [title] *Kreika* [name]. From what he said, if we were to say we were a "region patrol ship" [*Sagefuda:*[13] The "patrol ship" mentioned herein also appears in a newspaper published in Britain. I have translated a separate extract.] and procured a supporting letter from the local authorities, we should meet with no difficulties on our journey. Golovnin was able to receive such a letter from a British official called Secretariat [title] *Kanishika* [name][14]. [Translator's note: Regarding the matter of the Russian officials posted in London mentioned in this section: It seems European law permits allies to station one or two officials each in each other's country. Additionally, even if a "region patrol ship" should encounter an enemy ship it is never seized; this is a common law of Europe.]

12.

During Captain Golovnin's stay in London, vice-captain Rickord met a man

---

[13] Carlander: A *sagefuda* ("hanging note") is a separate note attached to a document, much like a tag on a string.

[14] Carlander: The placement and order of translator Murakami's explanatory notes "title" and "name" vary greatly throughout the document. Though many correctly identify which is which, or at least partially do so, many are also wrongly placed. While I would like to preserve as much of the original translation's character as possible, I have in this case – as with country names – chosen to assign what I to the best of my ability can establish as the correct definition and name.

called *Fronoum,* a British *hiliwaum* agent. According to him, a Dutch ship had recently been seized by the British on its way back to Holland from Batavia, and the ship had then been given into their custody. Among the books onboard, they had found two letters concerning Nagasaki. One was a letter from the Dutch functionary stationed in Nagasaki addressed to *Kolos Benshioner* [title] *Sinmerberning* [name] in Holland, and the other one a letter to Krusenstern [the captain of the ship Rezanov came to Nagasaki on]. The first letter to Sinmerberning stated that since the Russian envoy Rezanov hadn't brought an interpreter with him when he came to Nagasaki, the Dutch had interpreted for him, but arranged it so that Russia's wishes would not be granted. By presenting the delegation in a bad manner, they claimed to have succeeded in their goal. The letter was a report that through such action, the trade relations between Holland and Japan had been strengthened. The language used in the second letter to Krusenstern had been difficult to understand, but it appeared to be a letter expressing the writer's feelings of affection for the latter. Fronoum brought these letters to Rickord and interpreted them for him. Rickord wrote a letter to report the matter to Russia. When he later requested Fronoum to add a postscript, the latter accepted, saying only that it would be a shame if rumors of this came to spread widely, since it would be Russia's disgrace that their important envoy had come without an interpreter and so fallen victim to the plots of the Dutch.

13.

After receiving Fronoum's letter, bills of exchange from Canton, the Cape of Good Hope [Translator's note: A region that became Dutch territory some years ago. When Holland was annexed by France it became French,

but recently it was seized by the British and is now theirs.] and other locations, as well as procuring various necessities, Captain Golovnin returned to Portsmouth. While doing so he witnessed a British vessel bringing in a captured Danish ship from Copenhagen. After this, more provisions, firewood and water were purchased and we set sail for Brazilia. Our stay in Britain lasted approximately two months.

On our voyage from Britain to Brazilia we were assailed by harsh winds and rain, with the consequence that we lost a barge and the ship's mast was damaged. While at sea we observed the island called *Matekue* and British, Batavian, and American ships. On the seventieth day we entered the port of *Ekararine* in Brazilia, where we procured provisions, firewood and water, and replaced the broken mast. Around mid-January we headed for Cape *Kormi* [name of a cape in southern Africa], but as we neared the cape violent winds and bad weather caused many onboard to fall ill. On top of this, the ship had sprung more leaks and so we had no choice but to return to Africa's Cape of Good Hope. During the voyage we saw the island called *Terislashidariska* and met with gales many times again. Thereafter we entered the port of Simon's Bay at the Cape of Good Hope. There the British Captain *Corebets* [someone Golovnin knows well] and a lieutenant [title] [name unknown] came onboard the Diana. Captain Golovnin explained that, "We reached Cape Kormi, but the violent winds caused us such difficulties that we came here," and requested that they let us "procure provisions, repair the damages to the ship, and care for our sick." Corebets immediately returned to his own ship, but returned with armed soldiers, saying, "Since Britain and Russia are going to war soon, this ship will be seized."

Captain Golovnin showed him the letter from the British official and told him that the Diana was a "region patrol ship," whereupon the lieutenant [title] [name unknown] accepted the letter and returned to his own ship, leaving two men behind on the Diana. Fearing that the British would confiscate any classified documents onboard, Captain Golovnin used this opportunity to hide or burn such papers. Later, an official from Kapstadt [the port closest Simon's Bay and where British officials are stationed], Commodore [title] *Lore* [name], came to Simon's Bay along with a Hirizouem [title]. They said they wished to know "what orders we had received from Russia's officials." But when we presented them with the papers we had received from the Department of Science they told us that, "Due to the flaws in the letter you gave to the lieutenant and the entirely confused geography of the papers from the officials, we can only give you permission to set sail after first inquiring with officials in Britain. Until then, you are to stay here. Word from home should come in about five months." Thus a British officer called Moody came to be stationed on the Diana as her guard.

14.

After this, many ships came from Britain, bringing with them an Admiral [title] *Barch* [name] among others. Approximately six months passed, but still there was no word. Captain Golovnin headed to Kapstadt, where he converted the bills of exchange he had gotten from the merchants in Britain. While there, he heard from Barch and merchants that "a reply from Britain seems to already have arrived. It says there are some suspicious points in the statements given by the Diana's crew, but since a letter has already been granted by mainland officials the ship cannot be seized on the command of

another British official. Hence no matter how long you wait, permission to set sail is not likely to be given anytime soon." Captain Golovnin considered the situation carefully: "There is no telling when the war between Britain and Russia will be over. Staying here will only result in the goods being spoiled by the blazing heat of this place. The ship too is gradually acquiring damage, and then there is the issue of having to pay the crew considerably more because of the remote location." He then consulted a higher up maritime official about fleeing the port. Incidentally, it is a common practice in places that have two ports to change the port you stay in from year to year. [Translator's note: The port of Simon's Bay from May till October, and the port of *Strofe* from November till April. This may vary depending on the winds I am told.] And so ships began to head to the outer port, with even lead ships leaving harbor. Diana's guard, the British officer Moody, was ordered to board one of these lead ships as well and so departed. Thinking this was our chance, we prepared for our escape by procuring water, firewood, and – trying to be as inconspicuous as possible – all the provisions we could purchase. But the British official Admiral [title] Barch [name] saw this and told Captain *Tomkinsos:* "Captain Golovnin is not allowed to set sail without order. Keep possession of the documents given as proof." He was then sent to the Diana to notify us of this. Captain Golovnin reluctantly submitted a document under joint signature with the officer, stating that, "We are aware that escaping is a terribly shameful act in Europe." However prices gradually rose thereafter and with every day that passed the money we had on hand diminished. We were unable to procure fresh provisions, and neither were we given any by the British. Moreover, the damage to our goods was considerable. Captain Golovnin drew up a plan for our escape.

The ships that had been out on the sea were returning to port, making the number of vessels at anchor considerable. And so around the middle of May in year 1809 [around the middle of the fourth month in Bunka year six according to our calendar], Captain Golovnin wrote a letter to the Admiral, waited for a favorable wind, and left port. Out at sea we spotted a large vessel [country of origin unknown] in the distance. We frequently met with gales, making progress difficult. We stopped briefly at *Tana* Island [a small island which does not belong to any nation, Tana Island is located at approximately 165-6 degrees longitude, 16-7 degrees from the equator] where we procured provisions, water, firewood and the like. We reached Kamchatka around the end of September.

15.

While the Diana had been in the Cape of Good Hope a British war ship had also visited the region. It had been sent from Britain to plunder the villages built on the Russian territory between Kamchatka and America. After reaching Kamchatka, Captain Golovnin wrote a detailed report to the maritime officials in mainland Russia describing what had occurred since our voyage to Brazilia and the Cape of Good Hope, and the British war ship. What had happened at the Cape of Good Hope was something that would have incurred the anger of any king, but Russia's Emperors are often merciful and so usually accept all reasonable requests.

16.

The Petropavlovsk officials Captain *Mouchanov* and *Nitsune* were dispatched from Kamchatka. The *Hotsvokouniki* [title] *Siberiakov* [name],

along with then region officials Major general [title] *Koserev* [name] and Major [title] *Monakov* [name], as well as *Krubskoi,* were the previous officials in Petropavlovsk, but we heard that these were now retired. We also heard from the current official on this occasion, [title] Major general [name] *Petroskoi,* and the general manager *Harevnikov* of the Russian American Company that, "Khvostov and Davydov had been ordered arrested and imprisoned in Okhotsk for the acts of violence they committed on villages in Japan. Officials had questioned the crew of their ship, and the goods onboard had been sealed and put into a warehouse. Khvostov and Davydov escaped from their prison once, but were arrested again and sent to Petersburg. It was therefore assumed that they would be punished after a more thorough investigation there, but among their relatives they had persons of rank and pleas were made for their lives. To expiate them they were thus sent off to fight in the war with Sweden. There they left such excellent results behind them no matter where they were sent that, while they were not acquitted of their crimes, they are now employed as the staff of the aforementioned Siberiakov and *Mouchara.* There can be no doubt about this since they themselves said so."

Furthermore, the reason all vessels are currently being examined so carefully is because of this incident caused by Khvostov. From what I heard later on, it had been Rezanov that, unable to forgive the answer given to him by the Japanese officials, had verbally requested Khvostov to set out for and attack Japan with one of the Company ships. Captain Krusenstern apparently learned of this order and sent for Khvostov, telling him: "If you carry out the order given to you by Rezanov, you will be severely punished. I urge

you to reconsider." Khvostov apparently agreed to do so at this time.

Meanwhile, Rezanov loaded the goods he had tried to bring to Japan on to a company ship called Mariia and set sail for Novo-Arkhangelsk [name of a place in Russia's North American territory], accompanied by Khvostov and Davydov. Spending the winter there, he purchased a Boston ship called Juno [ship name] and had the goods from the aforementioned ship loaded onto this new one. Once again accompanied by Khvostov and Davydov he then set out for California [located South of the Russian American territory], where they sold all goods before returning to Kamchatka.

On this occasion, something of vital importance occurred to Rezanov, making him change his mind. Already upon departing Okhotsk he had sent Khvostov a written order to by all means call off the voyage to Japan he had previously ordered and telling him that no more indiscreet acts must be made. Khvostov gave his agreement to this, but when he later spoke to a sworn friend, he told the other: "It is nothing to mourn; should the sheep surrounded by turnips eat some of them, it ought to be forgiven." [Translator's note: This is a Russian proverb, saying it is no use to mourn any lost turnips if one, knowing sheep are fond of eating them, still left the enclosure open and came back to discover them gone. Khvostov thus meant to say that it was too late for Rezanov to call things off now when he had even provided him with a ship, knowing full well that Khvostov had a love of fighting.]

Khvostov thus began his first attack. What lies he told upon returning to Kamchatka not even the officials knew, but it was not until the end of that winter that Major general [title] Koserev [name] became aware of the truth

of what Khvostov had done and thought to arrest him. Khvostov's friend apparently sent word of this to him, though, and so despite the fact that it was early spring and the sea was still frozen he broke through the ice and fled. Because they had failed to arrest Khvostov, Major general [title] Koserev [name] along with the Petropavlovsk official Major Monakov [name] and Rovskoi were all three stripped of their offices.

Khvostov and Davydov went on to attack Japan a second time after that, after which they stopped by Okhotsk to find out what might be good to bring with them to America. Though they carefully hid their crimes, one of the men handling their onboard goods called *Nishashnikov* got drunk and revealed the whole story of the violence they had committed as well as everything else, leading to the local official Bokovniki [title] *Vuhalin* [name] learning of the matter. Summoning Khvostov and Davydov before him, he found proof of the attacks and arrested and imprisoned them both, confiscating and sealing all the goods that had been onboard the ship. The two Japanese who had been onboard were freed and an order given to place them under heavy protection. However, since the Okhotsk region is plagued by bad weather on top of being marshland, there was concern the goods plundered in Japan would soon be damaged if they were left in storage. The official named *Vavaev,* come to the region to relieve Vuhalin, communicated the wishes from the general manager at the Company, having a relation in the Company himself. Among what was said was that while there should have been orders from the imperial capital regarding Khvostov's cargo, no instructions had been received. Yet leaving the wares in the warehouse like this would cause everything to rot. The goods would become unfit to return

to Japan. On top of this the Company was already troubled by the losses it had incurred time and again. In the case they were to give restitution they would therefore do it in the form of money or wares of a kind, and so wished to please be given permission to sell off the goods as well as to have word sent to the Irkutsk officials on their behalf.

[Translator's note: Regarding the arrest of Khvostov in Okhotsk described in this passage: according to *Shashinikov,* Khvostov and Davydov were immediately summoned after the other local officials had given their consent. When questioned about their intended destination, they lied that they were sailing to Japan to do a bit of trade, and were consequently restrained. When some lesser officials conducted a search of their ship, the presence of two Japanese was discovered, leading to the truth of the matter being quickly exposed.

∘The relation of Vavaev's mentioned in this section is his wife's father, a merchant in the company.

∘The repeated financial losses mentioned in this section were those the Company incurred when it had to accept responsibility for and handle the consequences of the actions of its employees, Khvostov and Davydov. In addition to this the goods onboard the ship had not only been things plundered from Japan, but also included Company goods. These had been sealed away during the confiscation process as well, resulting in an overarching loss for the company.]

It was under such circumstances that the two Japanese, not knowing when their stay in Okhotsk would come to an end and thinking only of returning home, were compelled to purloin a riverboat and flee during the night, going missing. Besides these two, it is said some Japanese escaped the Kamchatka region via the Kurile Islands, though it is unclear how many and the matter has not been investigated properly. However the Kuriles claim to not have seen anyone like that, and the people in Kamchatka speculate whether they did not go down at sea.

17.

The unfortunate Rezanov [Translator's note: It seems Moor phrased himself thus because Rezanov had, despite traveling to Nagasaki, been unsuccessful in getting his application for trade granted, and after his return home felt such anguish over how things had ended that he died.] sent a letter of confession to the mainland officials on his way home, begging them for forgiveness. He repeatedly sent messages asking them to "please forgive him," but shame made him deeply regret what he had done and in the end he passed away in a place called Krasnoyarsk. Then there was Rezanov's relative *Galawachov,* a man of good lineage and remarkable intellect who had served as lieutenant while Rezanov had been onboard. It is said that when the Nadezhda returned to port, he shot himself out of shame over the outrageous actions of Rezanov, having first written down everything he had seen and experienced at Saint Helena Island. [Regarding the matter of Rezanov's death mentioned herein: One theory has it that he died from taking poison, but this is an unconfirmed rumor. It is difficult to say for certain, but the drug he supposedly used was *opicon,* one taken by those who have decided

to end their own lives. Taking the drug makes you unable to stay awake and you lose your life this way.]

[*Sagefuda*: Regarding the death of Galawachov mentioned in the above section, his name can also be found in the Captain's directory of names, which I have translated and submitted separately.]

As mentioned earlier, though Khvostov and Davydov performed great feats during the war with Sweden, they were never acquitted of their charges. And so in the end their troubled lives came to an end when they drowned, drunk, in the Neva River.

As for the Diana, the part of her cargo that was to be left in Kamchatka had all been unloaded. Moreover, the Bostonians had been ordered to come to America too, and we had heard that British warships were coming to the region as well. Having no other choice we thus set sail for America when spring came. Golovnin himself knew of the improper conduct of those in America, but thinking to gloss over earlier mistakes, he told the officials everything that had happened thus far. Moreover, given the Diana's mission to survey the Kurile Islands, the voyage came at quite a convenient time. However, considering that this was the first long distance voyage in some time for those onboard, Golovnin was reluctant to spend too much time surveying while at sea. And so, in order not to dampen everyone's enthusiasm about returning home, he chose not to say anything at all of these orders to those onboard. I heard this from Captain Rickord as well as from others. What do You now think of what Golovnin hid and I have said herein? Sure-

ly there has been nothing to be ashamed of.

18.

In the spring of 1810, the Diana set sail for Novo-Arkhangelsk. While at anchor there, ships from North America and Boston came in, and from what those onboard these told us, a British warship would be coming from Canton to the Russian territories in America. When it touched shore at some islands called the Sandwich Islands many of its crew had apparently run away, which along with the number of sick crew members had forced the ship to return to Canton again. There it had taken on new crew and the plan was to set sail for America and Kamchatka the coming year, or so we heard. The Diana returned to Kamchatka September that year. [The translator's note: The "Sandwich Islands" mentioned herein are located on a northerly latitude about 20 degrees from the equator. They have a warm climate and a rich variety of produce. The inhabitants are said to have come from Old Europe, but the majority presently consists of those born on the Islands. On the islands, there are tribe chiefs who act as supervising officials, caring for their people. Apparently it happens that the crew onboard the European vessels that stop here decide to stay on the Islands rather than return home.]

19.

The spring of that year, the Neva returned from America. I will record here what I heard from Lieutenant [This position can also be found on merchant ships. Their duty is to observe the weather.] *Kagenmeister* who travelled aboard her. The Neva had set sail from Cronstadt at the end of October in 1806 [the year before the Diana sailed from Russia] after taking on provi-

sions, water and firewood. They had touched shore at Brazilia's San Salvador, Hollandia Nova's[15] [New Holland] *Holtshakilin* [the name of a port in said location] and other locations before returning to port in Novo-Arkhangelsk in the summer of 1807, where they handed over their wares from the mainland to the local chief official, Baranov, and spent the winter. In 1808 they were given various goods to trade in Canton by the same Baranov, but word came from Okhotsk that war had broken out between Russia and Britain, and so their voyage to Canton was cancelled. From there they went to the Sandwich Islands, where they traded local produce, salt and other such wares and spent the winter. In the spring of 1809, they brought these goods back with them to Kamchatka, replaced their cargo, and returned to port in Novo-Arkhangelsk. Later they again loaded the ship with cargo in Kamchatka, but it was autumn and the winds were unfavorable, so they changed their plans and set sail for an island called *Kashiyaka* [located among the Aleutian Islands, I am told], where they wintered. They returned to Kamchatka in 1810.

When the Neva came to Novo-Arkhangelsk for the first time in 1807, the one who handled the onboard cargo had been a man called *Trovogilichkoi*. He was onboard the Neva also on this occasion, and when I met him he turned out to be an exceedingly pleasant and witty fellow. From what he told me, they had visited Kitaichina, Japan, and the Sandwich Island among other places. When I said that I would like to hear more in detail about all of this, he told me the following: Trovogilichkoi had sailed to Canton to-

---

[15] Iwashita: Present day Australia.

gether with the North American [Boston] captain *Wogein* after loading cargo on to the latter's ship. Once there it had been only Wogein who handled the trading since Trovogilichkoi had been unable to make himself understood. Upon returning, however, he apparently deceived Baranov as well as Trovogilichkoi. He was therefore denied when he later asked Baranov for new wares saying that he wanted to sail to Canton to trade again. It was during this time that Rezanov travelled to Japan as an envoy, failed to get his permission request granted and was told that Japan would not agree to any trade. However in order to get his hands on new cargo, Wogein worked out a scheme, apparently telling Baranov, "While Russian ships cannot currently call at Japanese ports, it is said that North American ships sometimes stop at Nagasaki. If you give me the cargo, I will travel to Japan without fail and trade it there before returning." Being ignorant of all such things Baranov believed Wogein and gave him the cargo. Bringing a cargo handler [the aforementioned Trovogilichkoi] and a letter for the Japanese officials and such with him, Wogein anchored in Nagasaki. While there he was among other things questioned about his reasons for coming to Japan. To this he promptly replied that he was only telling the truth when he said that a ship from America would – even with provisions stored onboard – run short if it tried to touch port in Europe. Uneasy about his prospects at sea he thus wished for them to please give him provisions. By way of compensation he would give them American products. The Japanese government office answered that, "provisions would be given to them, but no wares can be accepted."

Wogein thereafter sailed to Canton, where he did some trade and appar-

ently once more lied about prices to Trovogilichkoi. On his way back he touched at Kamchatka and unloaded half of his cargo there, taking the rest with him to America. It was after this that Baranov discovered that he had been fooled, but by then it was too late to do anything. Wogein later returned from Novo-Arkhangelsk, but his vessel sank, forcing him to stay in Novo-Arkhangelsk for a long time. Unable to do any type of trade he repeatedly asked Baranov for help and so became an employee of the Company. Feeling sorry for him, Baranov also gave Wogein a ship. However the boat flooded and sank at sea while on its way to an island called Kashiyaka. The crew survived by swimming ashore. Wogein and his wife resolved to abandon ship and went ashore too. That night a light was seen out on the ocean but it quickly disappeared and the next morning Wogein had no clue as to where the ship had disappeared.

As for Trovogilichkoi, he told me he had been ordered onboard the Neva the first time she sailed to Novo-Arkhangelsk. After that he sailed to the Sandwich Islands.

20.

The winter of that year, a letter came from Petersburg but no commands were given. However, the Okhotsk official called the *Hotsvokouniki* Minister [name] later brought with him a letter saying to sail the Diana to Okhotsk and to give a report of everything to Petersburg. Then in the early spring of 1811, written orders came from the mainland officials. The Captain was to sail for America, and we were to prepare accordingly. The letter confirmed that the Emperor had been informed by a naval official called *Desorverse*

[name] of what the latter had commanded the captain, and what the captain had reported about the surveying, upon which His Imperial Majesty had given His permission. Our orders were thus to survey the area between the Wovotska region located at 53 degrees and above and the Shantar Islands [name of islands], as well as the southern Kurile Islands. Written directives and maps would be provided at a later date. We also received a letter from an official in Wovotska on this occasion, saying that since the survey would surely not end quickly, we should return to port in Wovotska to be supplied with new provisions if we ran short. The money for miscellaneous expenses and various allowances was to be received from the Kamchatkan official *Petroskoi.* And so it was that I saw our twin[16] for the first time when we came to Kamchatka. The meeting went as described below.

21.

Around the end of that winter [around our calendar's New Year], the *Kamchatar* people [general term for the foreigners living in this region] spotted some unfamiliar looking people while out hunting. Bringing them back with them to a nearby village, they were told that they were Japanese. The Kamchatar people joined efforts to take care of them, and when they notified the government office, the *Generau* officials were ordered to put together a small unit and set out with a sled. There were four Japanese, all with injuries, and so they were brought back to where the government office was and treated there. When later asked about what had happened to them,

---

[16] Carlander: A likely reference to Diana's sister sloop, the Neva.

they said that their boat had been wrecked while sailing from Japan to Matsumae. They had lost their rudder and mast, and after drifting on the winter seas they had finally washed ashore in the Kamchatka region. Several people had drowned. Those who made it ashore had gone north, not knowing where they were. Shivering horribly and exhausted from starvation, some of them died. The remaining four then turned back south, where they met the Kamchatar people and were brought to their village. When asked about the cargo on the wrecked ship, they said they had been carrying sake. To confirm the truth of what they had said, the Generau, accompanied by some of their men, set out for the place where the dead and wrecked boat were said to be. Having navigated the craggy coast in the far north, parts of the boat along with clothes, rush mats, straw mats and the like were discovered in an inlet with two rocks called *Stowabe.* However the damage[17] had been completely buried in the deep snow and could not be seen. Continuing northwards, they found the bodies and buried them where they lay. On their way back they passed a freshly collapsed hill. Finding a Japanese straw mat nearby, they decided to search the collapsed cave by the shore. When they cleared away the fallen rocks and dirt they discovered three Japanese inside the cave. They had only narrowly escaped death. The Japanese were immediately taken care of, loaded onto the sled and taken to a port village. But horribly starved and injured in many places as they were, they have not yet been able to travel to where the government office is. I myself saw these four Japanese several times.

---

[17] Iwashita: The damaged body of the boat.

In this village, there is a dining hall in the home of the Grand Priest *Hiwora,* and there everyone is fed the same food as the priest. From what everyone says, one is a Buddhist priest, another a foreign trade merchant, the third a vice boatman, and the fourth a seaman. The other three are all seamen too, but it seems the boatman and others drowned when the ship was wrecked. The Buddha statue they brought along with them, the *roushi-ya*[18] and the Shinto priest have been placed in one location. Other decisions regarding the caring for the sick are left to the wishes of the Japanese; they are treated just like someone from our own country. Though they may be uneasy having washed ashore in a foreign land, I do not think they want for anything. I believe the magistrate's office too can rest easy in this regard.

22.

By the time we returned to port at Petropavlovsk to accept this money, it was the end of April. Since all of the Diana's preparations had finished we set sail the next day. As Captain Golovnin reasoned, the port in Okhotsk was difficult to enter except for during the summer, but waiting for summer would mean spending the spring idly[18]. Sailing for Okhotsk was thus not a favorable option. There were ports available among the Kurile Islands, though, and as we would likely need to procure more provisions, firewood and water, it was decided that we would sail from the Kurile Islands to the Shantar Islands and only circle the edges of the Okhotsk region, finishing

---

[18] Carlander: Possibly referring to Japanese prayer beads, juzu, which might have looked like rosaries (*rozarij*) in the eyes of the Russians.

the survey in one go before returning home. Considering the orders from the mainland, it seemed likely that peace would be concluded with the British troops before long, and so if we used our provisions sparingly we could make them last for about three months. And so we set sail for the Kurile Islands, thinking that wasting our time by sailing for Okhotsk would be unwise. However, because of the iciness of the sea we headed south first. [September, around the fourth month according to our calendar.] We were assaulted by violent winds and the ship took on water, spoiling much of our provisions. The number of rats onboard was unexpectedly large as well and they ate a good portion of the provision. Thereafter we sighted the islands of *Radawake* and Ketoi among others and thought to sail between *Raku-wake* and *Fushou,* but the tideway was too strong and we were forced back quite a bit by the headwind. Later we approached Ketoi again and I went ashore but found no inhabitants. After sailing around the island we sighted Shimushiru. After that we sailed to Ushishiri where the crewmember *Woldakov* went ashore, but as for what happened there it is just as I have already explained in detail in my testimony. [Translator's note: The written report submitted this past winter.]

On the island, Woldakov saw a copper kettle as well as pieces of cotton cloth and so asked the natives where they had procured these from. They replied that around the end of that winter, a shipwrecked vessel had been discovered in Shimushiru and they had found them there. Woldakov then asked where the ship had come from and how many the crew had been, but apparently they had all died in the water. The natives did not know where the ship had come from, but they were sure it was not a Russian vessel.

According to Captain Golovnin, Woldakov then surmised that the copper kettle and cotton cloth might have come from a British ship.

We then sailed around Rashowa Island and went ashore at *Yakoushiken.* When we spoke to the natives there they confirmed that what the Ushishiri people had said was probably the truth. They furthermore told us that the majority of the natives on the island lived in Shimushiru or Uruppu. A barge was then sent to Shimushiru, where it measured the depth of the harbor, but the fog was so heavy it was difficult to approach shore. We repeatedly lost sight of the island because of the heavy fog and the tide carried us away, making us lose our bearings. We sailed around Chirihoi Island, discerning its shore through the fog. We investigated the area using nothing but our charts, but since they indicated that it was the Island of Uruppu we turned our ship around and sent *Harevnikov* to Shimushiru's harbor *Wousero.* Having measured the depths of the water there the mouth of the harbor turned out to be very shallow and the Diana was unable to enter. Yakoushiken then went ashore in a barge to gather some vegetables. This time, while there were no natives, the remains of a pit of the type found in dwellings could be seen. In it he found the sail of a ship, but it was not of the kind used in Europe.

After that we sailed to Uruppu thinking we'd anchor in the harbor there, but the thick fog made it impossible to tell the islands apart. With the mountains and shore only slightly visible we could not distinguish any of the islands. The fog thinned briefly at one time and we could see a bit more clearly, but the Diana was already on their periphery and so we did not

know which ones they were.

[*Sagefuda*: The Harenikou mentioned herein is the same person who until now has been called Reunikou. When translating this letter on this occasion the name was spelled Harevnikou and so I translated it thus.]

[*Sagefuda*: Regarding the shipwrecked Shimushiru vessel mentioned herein, it was apparently quite a large ship painted entirely in red. As for what the Ushishiri natives had said were pieces of the sail, when Moor saw them for himself, all except for what had been found at the place in question appeared to be a type of fabric very similar to that used when making the soles of sown socks.[19] Furthermore, the shape of the kettle which had first washed ashore was no different to those produced in Britain. It seems Moor wrote in detail about this matter thinking that these types of objects might also be found on a Japanese ship.]

When we checked the charts to confirm whether it might be Uruppu, we saw that there a note had been made of an island between those of Uruppu and Etorofu. We could also see a tall mountain in the south and as the fog cleared it appeared as if the island split in front of the mountain. We all came to the conclusion that the island furthest away had to be Etorofu. On the island closer to us we could see small boats and huts made of grass as well as fields and such. Golovnin ordered me to go ashore and inquire about

---

[19] Carlander: The word used here is *tabi* (足袋) which usually refers to Japanese toe socks, but can also mean western ones. It is unclear which Moor thought it might be.

the name of the island, as well as its harbors and food. I took a barge to shore, and it was there that I first learned that the island belonged to Japan. When I later asked the Kuriles and Japanese, I was told that this island was Etorofu. I was greatly surprised. The interactions that we had thereafter with the Japanese officials I have described in a previously submitted report, and will therefore omit here.

When we first came to Kunashiri and Golovnin went ashore, we had the Etorofu officials' letter and harbored no treacherous intentions whatsoever, and the actions of the Kunashiri officials were not arbitrary either. Later they came bearing weapons, and looking at the drawings placed in the barrels sent out on the water while recalling what the natives had told Golovnin, we could clearly understand their intentions. When we later went ashore, it truly felt as if I had returned home, and we had no intentions to deceive anyone. However when the Kunashiri official then said that he would give us provisions but that the amount would depend on how many we were, Golovnin exaggerated our number in order to receive extra provisions. The official also asked us on this occasion whether we knew what Rezanov had been told by the Japanese when he came to Nagasaki. Since we did not understand the language and possible miscommunications would only cause suspicion, we answered that while we knew that Rezanov had sailed to Nagasaki, we did not know what he had been told or what had happened thereafter.

23.

While we had not received permission when coming to Japan, neither had

Britain when the Englishman Broughton[20] came to Matsumae some years ago, and we had heard from him that he had been treated very cordially. Moreover, a book with a detailed account of his visit has even been published. Judging by the treatment we ourselves received at Etorofu and the actions of the Japanese officials there, the book seemed to correspond well with reality. And so we were very glad to set sail for Kunashiri. However there the response of the officials was remarkably different and we were at one time forced to selfishly take food for ourselves. We were later reassured by the exchange of questions and answers that we had with the officials through drawings, having no idea that we were being lured into their net. And so we were arrested in the end and harshly treated. It was indeed quite an ordeal. After, we were locked up in a jail and questioned in detail about Khvostov's false documents and the testament of the Kuriles among other things. At this point we began to lose spirit, believing our wish to return home impossible. We resigned ourselves to our fate, but still we longed for Russia. Chivalry as well as wit turning into ignorance, we said that we would escape, but gradually even this talk died out. However, around the end of that winter [the first month of our calendar], they began to want to escape again and so I listened in on their conversation in secret, hearing them say that they would leave the biggest obstacle – Alexei – behind. Having been ill treated by this Alexei before and not knowing what fate would await me if things went according to their plan, I grew fearful. Unable to

---

[20] Iwashita: William Robert Broughton (1762-1821). Sailed to Yezo in 1796, and visited the village of Etomo, today called Muroran. He surveyed the coastal area of Yezo, and named the *Funkawan* (噴火湾) (also called the *Uchiurawan*).

bear the thought of betraying my companions, I considered the situation again and again. Until that point I had gone against the Captain's wishes, making him leave me out of things. Believing I would no doubt reveal their plans of escape to the Japanese, the Captain became uneasy and reminded me of old times, trying to persuade me that nothing had changed. Yet even after asking him directly I could not guess at his thoughts. He also told Alexei about all of this, earning his understanding and arranging it so that Alexei and I would think badly of each other, bearing the disgrace of spreading falsehoods.

[Translator's note: Regarding the betrayal of his companions, it seems Moor used the word "betray" since letting the Japanese know of their plans would result in him alone being seen as innocent while the others would be judged as villains. As for the Captain reminding him of the past, he apparently recalled that though he had been the commander in chief onboard the ship, and none had gone against his orders, Moor had gradually begun to refuse to do as he'd told him.]

Such being the circumstances, the Captain rejoiced greatly when I asked him about the escape. When I asked what they planned to do about Alexei, he answered that they would leave him behind. In response to this I told him that it was because of us Russians that Alexei had been forced into this difficult situation, and had so pitifully resigned himself to his fate. It would not do to leave him alone behind and make him our sacrifice. I suggested leaving a message behind to clear his name. And so I wrote a letter expressing our thanks for all the kindness we had received so far, as well as to ask that

Alexei please be returned to Rashowa since he was innocent. However, I learned various things following this and so burned these documents, telling the Captain that judging by Alexei's current state, it would be good to tell him of these plans.[21] And so I persuaded Alexei and we conferred about a great deal of things. We have until now joined forces to prevent the Captain's plots. Not knowing what his plans were, we arranged it so that, like guards, I kept watch during the day and Alexei at night. Later I warned the Captain that escape would be difficult. After that the Captain complained on every occasion that my conduct was wrong, making me angry, but even then I could not bring myself to tell the Japanese that my companions were planning something wicked. Having no other way to stop them I simply continued to say the same thing. Later, when I asked Vasiliev about the escape, I heard he had notified Simanov. Simanov then told me that they intended to escape by digging their way out from under the prison. Since Alexei and I had been made aware of this, we reassured them no such thing would happen. And so though they all suspected me and called me a coward I dealt with things in this way, having no other choice. My definition of cowardliness was different from theirs it seemed; they most likely thought it preferable to end their lives after having escaped and been brought back, and been made to endure the shame of having to face the magistrate's office. But if one is to end one's life then doing so in jail as an innocent man would bring less shame. Even if they did escape and survived, surely their shame would

---

[21] Carlander: This passage is considerably fractured in terms of logic and sentence structure, making it difficult to pin down exactly whose actions Moor is speaking of. This translation is just one interpretation of how the gaps may be filled. Professor Iwashita's interpretation differs in how he believes that it was Golovnin who burned the documents written for Alexei's sake. This might have been done in response to Moor's failed attempts at persuasion.

be tremendous. I believe one cannot call those who escaped from prison in this manner simply "obstinate."

24.

Not only I but also Alexei told the Captain and others the following at every opportunity. In the petitions and reports we had submitted to the magistrate's office we had even given our word to God. Why would they write such things if they intended to escape now? Why would they flee when the Japanese officials showed us kindness daily? I tried to persuade them but they would not listen. I could only think of the war that might ensue if a Russian ship came for us this year but did not to find us here. But I was unable to rid them of their wicked thoughts, and so they forgot the kindness we had been showed, their duty, and their reason. Thereafter the Captain came to me saying that it would be spring soon, and asked if I would not flee with them, so I told him that I had absolutely no intentions of doing so. And why rush when we had given our reasons and the petitions and reports we had submitted thus far had been accepted by the magistrate's office? Moreover, they had only treated us with ever increasing mercy, so why escape, I argued. If the Captain did flee, my head would be a fitting atonement. I told him that all would happen according to God's will, and if that meant I was to die then I was prepared for that. The Captain then said that since I was opposed to the idea, he would give up the thought of running away together, reassuring me some. However when I asked Vasiliev more closely about this, it seemed no one had been considering escape at that time.

Meanwhile, the magistrate's office changed our place of detention in

April [the third month according to our calendar], displaying even greater charity. He also granted some requests we had made, making me feel both grateful and joyous. However for a long time I received no commands. Had I been instructed to tell if there was anything I was mindful of, I was prepared to do so and right or wrong reveal what was in my heart. And so I only waited for an order, but my companions said nothing at all about escaping. As they have said while on the *oshirasu*,[22] they were secretly storing food, little by little each day, and hiding this from the guardsmen as well as the sailor(s) and myself – I suspected nothing at all.

25.

Around the middle of April [the third month in our calendar] the Captain told me after some thought: "If a Russian ship comes this year, and the Japanese do not hand us over to them, then I believe war will be inevitable and we will be imprisoned yet again. And what would our prospects be then? I think it best to escape after all." To which I responded: "I do not know whether there will be a war or not, but I do not think it likely that we will be put back in prison hereafter. Moreover, even if you do escape, this is an island country and the Japanese are no fools. You will soon be arrested and then what face will you show them on the *shirasu*? And what about the so sincerely written petitions and reports, or how you have given your word to God?" I said to persuade him.

The captain then said, "It is still too early; we cannot escape now. I am

---

[22] Carlander: Oshirasu, shirasu (御白州) - an area of white sand in a law court where suspects or witnesses were summoned to be tried or questioned by the magistrate.

not even considering it. However, it won't do to lose our spirits. I will make sure to tell them of this." To which I answered: "Even if I grew dispirited at this point, I will not run. All will happen according to God's will." The Captain as well as the others agreed with this.

When the talk thereafter turned to war, I said, "We are not yet on the frontlines and sooner or later the Japanese will develop too and we will see our homeland again as peace is made." This seemed to have reassured them all. In truth, I was probably the one who was most relieved of all. Thinking back on it now, they must have been pressed for time to cite dispiritedness and moreover accept what I had said just then. When I spoke to them there-after they seemed to have reconsidered their wicked thoughts, making me let down my guard. Then, on the twenty-third day of that month [corre-sponding to the twenty-fourth day of our calendar], they came back,[23] and to a man we went to bed at the fifth hour. Worn out, I fell into a deep sleep. The next morning when Fukumatsu woke myself and Alexei, he told us that the Russians had escaped. I hurried out of bed, surprised and confused. All had been for naught. I truly became like a madman then. I find it hard to speak of how our companions deceived and left myself and Alexei behind, and I am at a loss as to how to explain such an insult. In the end their actions were unforeseen, as I have said before. But now that it has come to this I can only blame my own carelessness. No matter what punishment is handed down, I can give no excuse, nor will I resent it.

---

[23] Carlander: Golovnin mentions in his Narrative that he and the others were often allowed out on walks around the general area. They used these opportunities to scout for boats and possible escape routes. They had been out walking also on the day of the escape.

26.

I have now presented this document, but I would ask of you to please collate and read it together with the reports I have previously submitted. I believe there may be some small differences, but if the magistrate's office gives it careful consideration they will surely see that it is all the same, and that I have only omitted the insult[24] in order not to cause suspicion, and likewise so with the matter of the number of people with wicked intentions growing. But though they may have had wicked intentions, they are in no way evil men. As for the imprisonment, I heard of it later, but it was the lies of the Kurile[25] in addition to Khvostov's attacks and Japan constantly doubting Russia, that made me worry about revealing that we had been surveying and keep quiet until now. Furthermore, we knew well what Rezanov had been told in Nagasaki and so we did not in any way come to Kunashiri to ask for help.

27.

As I have told You, while my distress has been allieviated by the fact that they could not escape, and that they all returned safely by the grace of God, I still cannot stop worrying. The attacks by Khvostov have caused the Dutch to bear a terrible grudge and Japan to be on guard against Russia. Adding to this my companions now escaped, lending all the more credence to what the Dutch in Nagasaki say. It pains me greatly to think of how this must have

---

[24] Iwashita: The matter of Golovnin's escape.

[25] Iwashita: Alexei.

made even the people who doubted the Dutch believe that Russia is a bear or a barbarian, a country without either honor or law. [Translator's note: The "bear" in the above section is an idiom in Russia and has the same meaning as "beast" does in our expression "like a beast." It is a metaphor for a most brutal person, and is different from other expressions using cats, dogs, foxes, or tanuki.]

28.

To return the great charity of the Magistrate's office and officials with evil, forgetting the mercy shown to us, is inexcusable. No one, unless they have met with extreme hardships, can understand the anguish that fills one's breast or the thoughts of home that cannot be forgotten. In a time of moderate trouble one can still make prudent judgments, but if the circumstances become too much then matters are considerably different. Day and night you sink into despair, and as your fate grows tenuous, your thinking and wits are clouded, and you long only for the peaceful days of old, turning ever more ignorant. Only those who have experienced such troubles as we have can comprehend these feelings. It is only because I am in my prime that I did not do what they did. To judge all Russians by my companions who escaped would therefore not be accurate at all. Russia may span vast regions, but the whole nation is ruled by the same laws and if there is a wrongdoer he will sooner or later be punished. Russians are neither bears nor barbarians: they are still men.

29.

In truth, it is well known even in Europe that Russia excels in military matters.

[*Sagefuda*: That mainland Russia would excel in military matters is simply what Moor claims, but he states that it was written so in the separate notes in the extracts of the correspondence sent home by soldiers during the battle of Sweden and Finland.]

For instance, on one occasion in year 1805 [the third year of Bunka according to our calendar] when a Russian General-Kniaz [a nobleman's title] called *Vokrachiona* [name] was garrisoned along with 8 000 men, he was surrounded by 33 000 Frenchmen. He told his allied troops: "There are only two choices: to be taken prisoner, or die in battle." To this the soldiers responded, "We can only wait for an order to be given. We made peace with the thought of dying a long time ago," and rushed the French troops. Many of them died in battle, but in the end twenty French soldiers were taken prisoner, the battle was won and they returned to the headquarters. [Translator's note: The battle mentioned in this section seems to have taken place in the region of Germania. The "headquarters" mentioned were those of then supreme commander *Kotobuv.*]

However, these French are well versed in the art of war. Moreover, that chivalry is strictly observed in Russia is proven by Gawawachov's suicide. As I have explained previously, he took his life because he was related to Rezanov and felt horrible shame over the latter's unpardonable behavior. Besides this, duty and integrity are truly lauded in Russia, and the nation's laws prescribe sincerity and love for your fellow man. While it seems torture is being used even now in other countries, it is never done in Russia. As for what is written in the laws and ordinances about ten cases where guilty

can be pardoned, in the case of someone who has until then never committed any crime, but killed an innocent, it is still properly written that they will be punished. Like with all humans, the minds of youths are like the metaphor of honey and wax. They are thus shown even less leniency when punished. From these things it can be said that Russia's teachings are in no way inferior to those of a country with teachings that date back several thousands of years. In particular, compared to other nations, Russia has the greatest number of *Cheloveko Lyubee Denya.* [Translator's note: This is a general term for hospitals, orphanages, and other institutions. It is also a government office that provides support for widows and other lonely people.] These days, the arts and technology are gradually developing, too – Russia is not lagging behind other countries in its development. I believe You have seen the gifts from the Emperor brought to Japan; these are but a few examples. And though I do not know the details – indeed even if I do say these things – you might not know it here in Japan, but any foreigner would know this well, and many books on the subject have been published. I would thus like to request that the magistrate's office consider all of this carefully when judging whether Russia is a barbarian or a bear. Because of the repeated examinations we have been put through, it appears to me that Japan seems to think of Russia as a country of killers, or one with a war-loving character. And further, that Russia intends to come to Japan's northern islands to claim them. Likely these concerns grew even further with the arrival of the plunderer Khvostov. And though the Dutch should have helped to eliminate such worries, I believe they are encouraging them instead. But these are all nothing but great misunderstandings, as is the claim by my companions after their escape that this was acceptable behavior. However,

Russia is as I have said infinitely wise and peace-loving, and while I may not have succeeded in dispelling these misunderstandings, I have now at least related the truth in brief.

30.

Regarding the matter of Russia declaring war on Japan, if one considers the advantages and disadvantages of doing so, then Russia would no doubt attack by way of Yezo, occupying the island. But I wonder what use it would have once taken. If Russia attempts to hold Yezo, how will she recompense the expenses incurred during the war, or the loss of so many lives? There will furthermore be the upkeep of the strongholds built all over, and death will be inevitable for many in this extremely cold frontier land, beginning with the guards and soldiers and the crew of the transportation vessels the guarding soldiers travel on these. What merit would these islands hold for the immense Russia? Russia's climate varies in temperature, but a multitude of produce is yielded in great amounts within our borders and on the contrary it is foreign countries that desire Russian land. How much produce does Matsumae or the Yezo Islands have? In most cases they are all things that can be procured in Kamchatka. Yezo produces much "bad fish"[26] besides yielding kelp, abalones, and sea cucumbers, but in Kamchatka a smaller quantity of "good fish" is yielded, enough even to send to Yezo or the like. Kelp, abalones, and sea cucumbers and such are not used for food in Russia. Besides these, Yezo has pearls, but the aforementioned inferior

---

[26] Carlander: Written as悪魚, the word is also an old synonym for "shark." Either Moor is comparing the inferiority / superiority of the fish produced in the waters he's speaking of, or he's actually meaning to say that the waters are filled with sharks.

goods are produced in great amounts in Kamchatka and the second island, too [meaning *Sasemunku*]. When there's nothing but a few dolphins, seals, deer, martens that look like cats, and foxes that look like dogs, then would Russia really be after this land? In the Kamchatka region, about a hundred thousand good deer and marten skins can be collected each year. Deer are kept in great numbers by all families.

Despite this Kamchatka is one of the Russian territories' extreme badlands, and Japan's Yezo is a poor region just like it. Because the circulation of goods is unrestricted in all of Russia, everyone is entirely indifferent to and pays no attention to Kamchatka and other such places. So why then would Russia and Japan go to war against each other? Russians have been visiting the Kurile Islands and Yezo since ancient times, and it was only recently that the Japanese began to gradually annex Yezo. No notice whatsoever was given to Russia of this, but it was known in Russia. Nevertheless, like I have said earlier, that two nations would go to war over – as the saying goes – a lean rock is not good. So what reason would Russia have to go to battle over this rock at this date? The Japanese probably think that only Japan knows of the produce and so on of Yezo, but I have known about it for fifteen years already and still things are as I have said. [Translator's note: The "lean rock" herein refers to the fact that since Yezo has no good quality produce it truly is like a rock. It seems Moor wrote thus meaning a "poor rock." The "rock" mentioned later on in the passage has the same meaning.]

31.

The people in Russia are not all bears or barbarians – there are also good men. Japan delayed its answer to our envoy,[27] and even deprived the envoy's attendants and soldiers of their freedom, but at home they quickly perceived the true intentions of Japan and felt no anger.

Being a very proud people, there was a time when the Chinese refused a Russian envoy, *Garaha Gorovkin* just like Japan did. Various officials at home quickly saw the unique traits of the Chinese, though, and bore the insult, sighing magnanimously. To war with China was our good fortune and no chore, but the Chinese soon gave a strict command and those who had refused the Russian envoy were punished it seems.

[Translator's note: The "guessed the true intentions of Japan" herein likely refers to what Moor wrote earlier, saying that news are difficult to communicate since Russia is far away from Europe.

◦"Being a very proud people, the Chinese…" Moor expressed himself thus recalling that the Chinese claim that their land was created by saints, and furthermore call other countries barbarian. The place where the Russian envoy attempted to hold negotiations was called Kyakhta and is located near Irkutsk. Due to the Russians' greedy desire for profit both parties had begun trading false goods more and more, leading to trade relations being

---

[27] Iwashita: Rezanov.

broken off all together in the end. This year, after Alexander succeeded the throne, Irkutsk officials again sought to conclude a general trade treaty with China. To negotiate the contents of the treaty the Russian official mentioned herein was sent as an envoy to Peking, but was stopped by the Chinese on his way there. The envoy hence returned to Irkutsk, but perhaps due to the strict command given by the Chinese, an envoy from China was sent to Irkutsk and it seems a trade treaty was concluded. To battle with China was in this manner Russia's good fortune and no chore, I am told.

Many breeds of martens can be found between this Kyakhta and the southern parts of the Amur River, and they are apparently of exceptionally good quality. If one were to occupy this region it would therefore benefit national prosperity considerably, and moreover, since the land is adjacent, transportation will also be easy. Overall there will be no difficulties it seems.]

32.

Because the Russian Emperor's ensign was subjected to such a great insult last year, if worse comes to worst and there is war this year, I do not think Russia can be blamed. Though there have thus far been no requests from Japan, Khvostov and Davydov have been punished according to the laws of our homeland and in a humanitarian manner. In this manner, matters are dealt with in a magnanimous spirit in Russia, but even this generosity has its limits. That I and my companions were sent to Kunashiri – even supposing we were sent because of our country's desire to wage war – must thus have been for a good reason, and so I think it best to have these battleships

returned unharmed. I am, however, not certain of the intentions of my country, and there has been no order for our return. Yet as I see it, while Russia is not fond of war, I believe Japan may be.

[Translator's note: The statement herein about the ensign being subjected to a great insult refers to how, despite the fact that they were in no way plunderers, they were treated as such, and how on top of this their Captain was ordered arrested, making it impossible for them to raise their ensign on the ship's mast no matter what port the ship was to enter thereafter. Of course, if it had been war and the captain was taken prisoner aboard the ship or died in battle, they would have had no choice but to lower the flag. It seems that this constitutes an insult to the emperor if the ship is one which has been named by him personally and even granted an ensign.]

33.

Regarding the aforementioned matters, whatever may happen here on after, what I say while I live will always be nothing but the truth, even after I pass. I therefore implore you not to condemn me. Only God knows that I tell no lies. The reason I write this document is hence not out of any wish for me and my companions to be ordered to return home but simply to inform Japan of the state of affairs in the West, which might possibly be of some use. I am a Russian soldier and certainly no barbarian. I am originally a free man, and I follow the way of honor of my homeland. I do not know the minds of my companions, or others for that matter, but I believe that it was unavoidable that the smaller things that were done were hidden, and so I have simply related here in all honesty the general course of events as they

took place. No matter what comes here on after, I do not wish for this.[28]

34.

Having gotten to know and understand the great intentions of the magistrate's office as well as those aided further by the officials, we request that Japan forget all it has previously believed and felt, and think of us Russians as fellow human beings. Disregarding danger, I have herein written everything honestly and left nothing out. I have of course from the start wished to clear suspicions and make it so that Japan and Russia can associate without differences. Whether they be good or bad I therefore humbly request that instructions be given to me soon. [Translator's note: I can confirm that this wish to quickly receive instructions is something Moor has expressed every time we have spoken.]

But then my companions escaped and the situation became one where permission to return home could no longer be granted. The other day I told the magistrate's office in all gravity that when I had written requests or the like before, I had only asked that we would be given permission to return home, but due to the others' escape, I could no longer make such requests. My sole reason for gripping my pen now is my sincere and wholehearted wish that our two countries be happy. And so at the risk of losing my life I have now recorded all that has been herein, including things that will bring shame to various individuals. I have thus abandoned chivalry, but it cannot be helped. There is nothing left for me to do but reveal all and die.

---

[28] Iwashita: To return to Russia.

35.

As I now speak, I do so feeling like a guilty child facing his father, ready to repent my wrongdoings for the rest of my life. As proof of my gratitude for the charity shown to us, I simply wish to describe the current state of affairs in Europe. I ask that you accept this document with this in mind.

36.

Answers have already been given for some of the questions that have been asked, but as it seems I still have not been able to convince You, I can only surmise that this must be the fault of the Dutch in Nagasaki, who seeking to further their own interests, have concealed the truth and spoken only ill of foreign countries.

[*Sagefuda*: Moor's discussion of this document's main issue concludes here. From here on he talks about the wars in Europe.]

This Holland was some years ago a dependency of Spain[29] and the two countries assisted each other in harmony. Moreover, the Dutch laws are very reasonable, and Holland is praised even in Europe for being strong-willed and refusing to listen to the orders of other countries. Though it is a small nation it has a prosperous trade and is well versed in naval warfare. Apparently, they are currently expanding their territories. But be that as it

---

[29] Iwashita: Holland became Spanish territory in 1556 and was later acknowledged as an independent state in 1648 in the Westphalia treaty.

may, it is said Holland's wealth is so great it defies measurement. Russia's late emperor Peter was a wise man and traveled various countries.[30] Dutch ways were even adopted in Russia and Holland came to be respected as a teacher. From there on our countries became allies and promises were made that this would never change. [Translator's note: The mention herein of Holland previously being allied to Russia is made in order to explain that Russia has never held a grudge against Holland, and that they only reluctantly became enemies when Holland was annexed by France. The unrest in France and its annexation of Holland will be discussed hereafter it seems.]

37.

Between the year 1791 and 1792 [fourth and fifth year of Kansei], great changes occurred in Europe because of the turmoil in France. France's laws, church and people were divided and finally in 1793 they killed their king and queen. The king's family and dignitaries tried to avenge them and those who had tried to support the old laws all fled the country. As a consequence of all this, various countries began fighting amongst each other and since they all made claims on sovereignty, the killing continued endlessly. Europe's countries began to resent the atrocities committed in France. In an effort to somehow revive the old laws everyone began to arm themselves with weapons, and in the end the French troops went to war against Germania, Prussia, Spain, England, Italy and others. Holland, too, fought against France, but just as when a great river overflows, the small ditches

---

[30] Iwashita: A Russian embassy was dispatched to Western Europe between 1697-98. Peter the Great himself joined as a member of the observation party.

and rivers were instantly crushed. France annexed these small countries and laid them all under obligations. Prussia laid down their weapons, Spain made peace and allied itself with France, and Italy surrendered, prostrating itself before France. Holland, however, still continued to fight. But with the help of providence, it too finally fell to France and all of its wealth was taken by the French. After this Holland would have preferred not to war anymore but they were forced to fight for France, and so their foreign territory and fleet suffered losses every time there was battle.

Germania was still carrying on the war and had thus gradually weakened. Because it bordered on Russia it was invaded by countries like Turkey, Prussia, and Sweden. Additionally, among the Bavarians there were those who, like the French, wanted the position of sovereign, and so it happened that the country's lords had to flee to Petersburg. There was much unrest like this but it was all suppressed and Bavaria surrendered to Russia.

Then in 1795, requests for relief came from Germania and Britain and warships were dispatched to guard Britain. At the time, France was in control of Sardinia [name of location], Venice [name of location], *Kreieski* Island [island located in the Mediterranean Sea] and Egypt [located on the African continent]. All became *alestabrikanskoe.* [Translator's note: A term for when a country has no sovereign and a political office for unification is established to carry out political decisions. It seems Dutch laws were all enforced in this manner in the past. The Bostonians were ruled by similar means.]

The name of France's current emperor is Napoleon. He used to be a lowly officer, but thanks to his talent for strategy he was promoted to the position of a high ranking one. Winning battles in Italy as well as Egypt, he returned home and rose to the office of First changing his name to Napoleon and surname to Bonaparte. [Translator's note: The consul mentioned herein holds the same authority as that of a king. There are however three people with this title and they are meant to jointly discuss the administration of the country. When the aforementioned Bonaparte came into this office the other two were such imbeciles that when Bonaparte became emperor he made them into nobility.]

With the circumstances being such, all of Europe came to Russia to request help after being impoverished. In year 1797, the late Emperor Pavel Petrovich [father to the current sovereign] mobilized the entire country's soldiers and had the general and official Feldmarschall administrator *Galahasuorov* prevent an invasion by France. This man made the French troops that had invaded Germania, Italy, Switzerland and other countries retreat, and returned victorious to Petersburg in year 1799. Russia also reclaimed the island called *Kerechieskiha* on this occasion since it had been taken by France. The name of the lord of this island was *Dersht* and on his request to Russia to "defend his home island" warships were dispatched for its defense. [Translator's note: The name of the first general to head to the Kerechieskiha mentioned herein was *Ushiyakou,* but he was thereafter relieved. A man called Shiniyavin was sent there next I am told.]

On this occasion, requests were made by the Dutch prince [a common

way of calling Russian daimyos] called *Wolanskako* as well as the British. Warships were dispatched, Holland was given assistance and a place called *Keuldern* [name of location] was occupied. The British defeated the French at sea. Then, because Russia and Britain were both unfamiliar with the geography, *Gelman* [a general in the Russian army] was taken prisoner by the French. After this a place called Arikimal was occupied, but gradually the Dutch's loyalties were changing due to France's manipulations. The people of Holland came to loathe having to support this prince and foreigners, and the realization of what had originally been intended became impossible. Consequently, a great number of people were killed and a fortune was spent under the leadership of the aforementioned prince and Junker [official title] *Yorkasko* [general in the British troops], but in the end they were forced to abandon Holland and return home. Britain, too, experienced the same thing. [Translator's note: At the time of the war described herein, Moor was 16 years of age and employed on the warship of Supreme Commander *Chichekov.* Because he was engaged in operations aboard he did not take part in the fighting, but he tells me he witnessed it in person.]

At this time, the British had taken control over an island called Malta. [Translator's note: I am told this island is located in the Mediterranean Sea.] Since this secured the provision routes of many countries, the French only reluctantly surrendered the island. From there on the British gradually drove the French towards the region of Egypt, and together with their frequent victories at sea this made them terribly conceited and they turned maritime customs from ancient times completely on their head, doing things like seizing ships from different countries.

[Translator's note: The maritime custom mentioned herein refers to the European custom of permitting the seizure of enemy vessels, but not non-enemy countries' vessels, which had been in practice until then. However, I am told that Britain has recently established a new law saying that they will be able to seize all vessels sailing for the enemy country, even if it is not an enemy one.]

38.

In year 1799, Malta's Lord *Delita* came to Petersburg, asking Russia to incorporate the island into its territories and defend it. The consent of France and other European countries were obtained after discussions, and so word was sent to Britain that Russia would take possession of this island. It was also communicated that smaller countries would not be made light of and that, unless it was an enemy one, vessels would not be seized. Furthermore, Russia would take possession of Malta. However, the British could not accept this order and replied that this would mean war. In the midst of all of this, Pavel Petrovich suddenly died in the beginning of spring year 1801, and just as *miroljovij* Alexander Pavlovich[31] [the current Emperor of Russia] succeeded the throne, the British warships quickly sailed to Copenhagen [the capital of Denmark] and attacked Denmark's unfortified areas causing a war to break out. The British forces were numerous, but Denmark took a strictly defensive stance and thanks to the great discretion of her prince [a common term for the daimyo of this country] all fighting was suspended.

---

[31] Carlander: The Russian adjective miroljovij (миролюбвый).

[Translator's note: The "roljovij" herein means to "love peace". After this Alexander was enthroned he engaged in and called for reconciliation whenever the European states made peace. He thus came to be called this other by all of Europe.

◦The "prince" of Denmark mentioned herein refers to the heir of the Danish king. "Great discretion" refers to the time when two large British ships drew near the Danish castle but were cornered in the shallow waters and became the target of heavy fire from the castle. The British sent a messenger saying that onboard the British warship there were many newly captured Danish sailors, and that if they destroyed the ship all of the Danish prisoners would die. The situation was one where if these two ships were sunk, the British forces would be vanquished, but the prince was fooled by this information about his own country's sailors and halted the gunfire. The British warships could then retreat with only minor damages. It seems enemies and allies alike were moved by the prince's merciful spirit and a truce was called.]

Hearing of this the Emperor of Russia sent a messenger to Britain saying, "To live in peace means to make no war." And so Britain finally made peace with Denmark and *Silecia,* were provided with water and provisions by Russia, and returned home. Being the owner of a generous and great heart, the Emperor feared losing numerous men over "a single island" [referring to the island of Malta] and in the end handed over what might as well have been an island in his territory to Britain. He thereafter sent requests to various European countries and took the trouble to call for peace between

all. Britain and Austria along with some others then met and after some discussion it was finally decided that peace would be made with France. All of Europe came to extoll the virtues of Alexander in this manner. In the ports of many seas only merchant ships began to pass through in great numbers, and all rejoiced, able to live in peace again. Even the poor could be satiated.[32]

When the war was yet not over, the French had written a peace document and a treaty was concluded. In the document they had written that they would return the occupied territories of Holland, Italy, Hanover [name of a country] and others to their previous owners. But now that France had claimed colonies all over the world just like Britain, it refused to surrender them like the treaty had promised. Peace was achieved, but they guarded the toured areas [referring to Holland, Italy and others] all the more fiercely and so inevitably war broke out again. In the year 1804, blood was shed in battle in many regions, and some places were even turned into rivers of blood. Saying he could not bear to watch, Russia's Emperor went to great pains and once more acted as an intermediary in peace talks between France and Britain, but nothing came of them. France was occupied only with the thought of annexing all of Europe, and so because of its relations and allies [Translator's note: Referring to Prussia, Austria, Sweden, and others I am told.] as well as disagreements with the territories it desired, Russia too was forced to take up arms and fight.

---

[32] Iwashita: "Could eat their fill."

[Translator's note: What is said in herein about France thinking only about annexing the whole of Europe can be found in books published later on. While it hardly needs saying, it would be the same as planning the annexation of the five worlds. After making peace with Russia, France sent word asking to please let them use its roads to send a great army to the Black Sea since they wished to invade Asia. However Russia did not give its consent and so no such thing came to pass.

As mentioned herein, Egypt, Africa, had already been struck and lost its freedom, and when all of Europe made peace many warships were constructed. Because their intention was to annex America, a simple seizure of a British ship came to spark a war. Thus this was not in any way limited only to all of Europe, for they intended to annex all five worlds. But not knowing the extent of this and believing that saying such a thing might on the contrary invite disbelief, Moor chose to write only "all of Europe."]

The Supreme Commander of France [referring to Napoleon] was then enthroned as emperor, and made his brothers lords of Holland and Italy. Then in the year 1805, a general from the Russian army called General *Anshef* [title] *Kotosov* came to Austria, travelling through the Kingdom of Prussia and arriving in Wien [the capital of Austria]. Guessing Austria's intentions and that Russia and Austria's generals were in disagreement, France first defeated Austria and then surrounded Russia's troops with tens of thousands of men. Russia's army suffered a crushing defeat, losing many soldiers, artillery and provisions. In the end they could do nothing but hold their ground. The commander in chief of the French army at this time was

Emperor Napoleon. Approximately a hundred thousand men died in battle, counting the soldiers of both armies. The number of fallen in the Russian army amounted to twenty-six thousand. Austria then implored Russia to please return home since Emperor Napoleon would not agree to peace if Russia did not leave Austria. And so the Russian troops returned home. The treasures in the Austrian capital, a place called Wien, were thereafter all seized by France. Francis III[33] [the name of Austria's king] succeeded in the difficult task of concluding peace, abolished the title of *Rimskako*[34] and took on the one of *Avshrariskako*[35] [a different name for Austria], or Emperor of Austria. [Translator's note: The "Rimskago" in this passage refers to the dozens of countries near Austria, together called the Muskako Union.[36] Germania occupies the seat of emperor of these countries.]

Furthermore, in the country there were people much like daimyos calling for the reinstitution of the *Reireskako* Union. These too separated and joined France, resulting in the loss of much land. France's victories gradually grew in number in this manner, and their desire to invade all countries grew stronger. Hence Britain and Russia did not encroach on Prussia even a little. Consequently, in the summer of year 1806, Napoleon defeated Prussia and sent word that by New Year Eve next year, they would be welcoming spring in Moscow [the former capital of Russia, previously called "Musu-

---

[33] Carlander: Francis II. It seems likely that Moor had the number confused when he wrote his report, saying the "third" instead of the "second". Furanchaf troi (フランチアフトロイ) in Murakami's translation.

[34] Carlander: Possibly coming from the Russian "римский король": roman emperor.

[35] Carlander: Possibly coming from "Австрии король": Austrian emperor.

[36] Carlander: The Holy Roman Empire.

kovia" in our country]. Because of this the forces in Russia were split up and in order to hinder their progress Napoleon sent messengers and gifts to Turkey, Persia, China and others, asking them to join him in fighting Russia. The frivolous Turkey and Persia thoughtlessly joined Napoleon immediately, but the essence of the answer China gave France was, "We made peace with Russia long ago, and have had no dispute with her. We have no intention of violating the peace agreement now. What reason would China have to go to war?"

Turkey and Persia were then gradually taught better in all fairness by Russia, but since they would not learn even Alexander lost his patience and said that he would take up arms. All of Europe's armies then gathered in Prussia, and it was only Austria that did not send any troops, worn out as it was from fierce battle with its pursuers and fearing that it would all lead to war. Thus in the year 1802,[37] the Russian army too settled along Prussia's eastern border as reinforcements for the Prussian army. The Prussian forces were all stationed along the western border. Then all at once the armies of France, Holland, Italy, Spain, Sardinia and Bavaria came bearing down and just like a frail little boat in a billow on the ocean, the powerful troops trained by the old king of Prussia were overpowered. Like smoke and fog disperses, so were they defeated near Jena [the name of a location in the Kingdom of Prussia]. Other than the Prussian ones there were no more reinforcements to be had and throughout the country people grew frightened and surrendered. To a one the people abandoned their villages and cities and

---

[37] Carlander: 1806. The War of the Fourth Coalition.

fled to Russia or Austria, leaving the country empty. As everything had been plundered by the French, from provisions to horses, the lord used a carriage to flee to Königsberg [name of a place in the Kingdom of Prussia, close to the Russian border].

The French army began its march on Russia thereafter. At first there was a Russian general called Feldmarschall Graf [title] *Kamentskii* [name], but because this person was sickly General *Ansef* Graf [title] *Beninkisen* [name] was made general, and there was some fighting but I do not know how much. Three decisive battles were fought near *Fuutosmaeshiishishiyu,*[38] Eylau and Königsberg. All three times Russia won, but more than half of the officers and soldiers died in battle. France and its allied countries' troops' number of fallen is said to have been more than four times that. Because of this, Russia ran short on provisions, and all its horses had been killed too. On top of this, the roads were poor and hardly anyone succeeded in returning home to Russia. [Translator's note: By the roads being poor, Moor means that this region turns into a great marsh when the snow thaws, and thus cannot easily be traversed. It is impassable except for during the hot or snowy season.]

Meanwhile, France had been plundering Prussia's storehouses from time to time since the start of the war and so had plenty of provisions. Starved and attacked from all directions, the Russians were engaged in battle wherever they went and became terribly exhausted. At a battle near

---

[38] Carlander: Possibly the twin battles of Jena-Auerstedt.

Friedland [location in the Kingdom of Prussia], both the enemy and allied troops were so fatigued that neither could take care of their injured. [Translator's note: Both armies were so tired from fighting that they could not even take them in.] Napoleon saw this and realized perhaps for the first time that he could not win all from Russia, and that he could not rely on Turkey, Persia and the others. Turkey had done some fighting, but only in a most feeble manner, and on that occasion lost Moldavia [place name] and the region where the river Don runs. [Russia won this region.] Persia lost Bakinsrie [place name] among many other territories [this too was won by Russia] and did nothing but flee so there were not really even any battles.

[Translator's note: This battle is a different one from the one described earlier. Since Turkey and Persia both had invaded, Feldmarschall [title] Gudovich [name] set out for Persia and General Ansera [title] Miiselson [name] to Turkey. The aforementioned and Bukseden [name] fought Turkey and Persia respectively and won it seems. As is described herein, it is said that they received a request from France in another battle. Moor included this as proof of Napoleon having understood that he could not depend on the other two countries.]

[Sagefuda: A letter sent home by an officer in the army after the occupation of the Don region mentioned herein can be found in a Russian newspaper. I will translate and submit this separately.]

39.

Napoleon requested to meet with Russia [Translator's note: this happened

the day after the battle of Friedland.] and when the two met they talked about concluding peace. It was decided much according to the wishes of Russia.

[Translator's note: The wishes of Russia mentioned in this passage refer to how the king of Prussia had already fled, and France occupied this region. The French said that they could not agree to peace if they had to return the land to Prussia's king. Alexander replied that if that was the case, they would have to fight again. I am told that France then accepted the terms. Other territories occupied by France were divided up and given to the Russian emperor. France had also taken secret British documents and the like, and it was decided that these would be presented to Alexander.

○This peace was concluded the year they sailed from their country and, as mentioned earlier, when they returned from Prussia. The one called *Kananshita* also returned after peace was made.]

Britain is an old ally of Russia's, but for a long time it has been Russia who has one-sidedly had to fight the hard battles, losing territory in distant places like Spain, France, Holland and the like. In recent years, however, Russia has tried to change its way of trading with Britain. [Translator's note: This refers to how some years ago, the British alone had come to travel as far as they wanted into the country and trade as they pleased. After becoming emperor, Alexander took on the task of changing this old way of trading, making it so that they could only enter through the port of Petersburg and prohibiting wholesale.]

Angered by how Russia had now proposed to make peace with France, they began to fight against Russia and her ally Denmark. Attacking Denmark's unfortified areas, they said to hand over all the lord's boats to Britain until peace could be concluded between all countries. But apparently Denmark did not accept and so half of the capital was set fire to, forcing the Danes to hand over their boats and military paraphernalia to Britain. [The battle in Denmark mentioned herein is the battle of Copenhagen that the Diana witnessed while at sea.]

40.

Being young and fond of war, Sweden's king created some truly troublesome situations, finally losing all of what is called Pomerania to France. The cannon fire that Diana heard while en route was in other words the sounds of battle from when the castle walls of the French Stralsund and Pomerania [all of these are the names of territories owned by Sweden] were decimated. The Emperor of Russia was related to Gustav[39] [the king of Sweden's name] and so frequently tried to persuade him to avoid this kind of war. He warned him that if he did not stop there would be war and he would end up losing even his country, but though this concern should have pleased the other, the hot-tempered king ordered Russia's envoy arrested and imprisoned. The envoy's residence was searched as well, and the documents found therein were copied and made public. [Translator's note: The envoy mentioned herein is the same one as in the previous passage; a person who is dispatched to allied countries. Among the documents that were found in his

---

[39] Iwashita: Gustav IV.

residence there were even secret ones that belonged to the Russian emperor, and when the king published these he was greatly humiliated.]

This was not only an insult to the envoy, but to all of Russia's emperors. Yet the gracious Alexander sent for the Swedish envoy [it seems one is always stationed in Petersburg] and told him, "Despite having treated your king cordially in all matters, he has acted outrageously in return. But even though We have been humiliated, you need not worry that We would respond in kind. You may do what you think best: If you wish to stay in Our country then you may do so, and if you wish to return to your country, then you may also do so whenever you wish. We are only ever thinking of the safety of your king, and now that peace has been made with France, We wish to forget the insult that was dealt us. And that is how matters are, so convey this to your king." When the envoy returned home, the escorting officials returned to Sweden as usual and requested to meet with the king. But King Gustav was young and the envoy was quickly put in prison. Bribes and a message were sent to Britain, saying that he wished for them to join his fight against Russia. After this Russia finally occupied Sweden's Finland [place name], an island called Gotland, Sveaborg, Åbo [place name], and so on.

Not only Russia but also the people of Sweden had come to realize that this king was not a good one. And so the people placed the king's uncle, the Prince [referring to a lord of this country] of Södermanland[40] [name] on the throne and the young king stepped down. Russia's Emperor was thereafter implored to agree to peace. Then in the year 1810, Russia made peace, and with the exception of the two places Sveaborg and Åbo, it returned all the

other land it had occupied. It is also said that it sent a great deal of provi-sions. [Translator's note: Regarding the country of Sweden mentioned here-in: Provisions were sent thusly because it is a place where food is hard to procure and because Sveaborg and Åbo had been occupied during the war.]

[*Sagefuda*: The occupation of Finland mentioned herein might also have been mentioned in a Russian newspaper sent home by an officer called Borg. I will extract, translate and submit it when I find it.]

Russia was greatly angered by Britain's outrageous conduct in Copen-hagen, but having exchanged documents of war they declared that a six month reprieve would be given, not only for the merchants and workmen who had come from Russia, but also for other vessels and for trade – from that of various goods, to house and lands – to be settled, after which they were to leave for Britain. Instructions were given to the Russian merchants as well: The British had been ordered to return home after a six months re-prieve and they were therefore to finish all ongoing transactions. They were told that an official would be assigned to everyone and so to refrain from disorderly conduct. Russia's discretion was truly great. [Translator's note: "Britain's outrageous conduct in Copenhagen" refers to how it – as has been described in an earlier passage – seized Danish vessels and military para-phernalia. Denmark is one of Russia's sibling countries, and Britain was

---

[40] Carlander: Karl XIII. The Duke of Södermanland. The "kako" at the end might like in previous examples be a shortened form of the Russian "король." Södermanland is thus not the name of an individual as Teisuke Murakami's explanatory note indicates, but one of a geographical region in Sweden.

still an ally at this time. Still, noting the places where fortification was lacking they then did as they pleased, inviting Russia's displeasure.]

I believe there were no bigger battles between 1807 and 1811. Britain seized the Speshnoy [Translator's note: The name of a government-owned Russian ship. It was in port when the Diana entered the same port.] in Portsmouth, and besides this, the fourteen-gunner *Wobena,*[41] [A government owned Russian ship. It was a small vessel with one mast.] unexpectedly encountered a large British ship loaded with forty-eight cannons near Revalia[42] [name of a port]. They engaged in battle for some time and many of the soldiers were killed. The official aboard only narrowly escaped death. But none of these were any greater battles. A Russian state ship loaded with seventy-four cannons was chased by two British ships near *Holg* [name of a port] in the Baltic [name of a sea], and one of them was bigger than the Russian vessel, but they engaged in battle for some time. Then, when over half of the crew had died and the sail had been torn, the ship finally washed up on a reef and got stuck so the crew had to go ashore and burn it. It seems the British did not land. [Translator's note: The story of the warship is something that happened after the Diana set sail, and something Moor learned of while in Kamchatka, I am told.]

---

[41] Carlander: There is a record of a 44-gunner, Opyt ("Experience"), being captured by the British in 1808.
[42] Carlander: Now Tallinn.

41.

France and Russia had made peace, but not all things went smoothly. For instance, France sent people similar to daimyos to places like *Weshchifutsu-mumi,* Württemberg, Saxony, and Bavaria [all names of places]. Besides this, *Wenenam* [geographic location], Austria's coastal area called the Adriatic, and the various countries in Italy's Roman region[43] [geographic location] were annexed by France. Following this, the place called Rome [location in Italy] was named the *vtorom gorodom*[44] [meaning "the Second Country"], and because Holland has some undesirable traits, half of it was administered by France while the other half was called Holland. However, after this they annexed all of it again. The French emperor gave Amsterdam [the largest city in Holland] the name tretsim *gorodom*[45] [meaning "the First City"]. [Translator's note: The sentence "Holland has some undesirable qualities" refers to how, initially, the French emperor's younger brother[46] was made king of Holland, but the emperor was enraged when the other adopted policies that went against his way of thinking, and so he first took away half of his kingdom, and then the rest of it. Furthermore, the two cities in the passage are called the Second and Third, and this is used as proof of one's own country I am told. The First City is the capital of France it seems.]

---

[43] Carlander: *Arimskue oblashichi* (アリムスクエヲブラシチ) in the Japanese translation.

[44] Carlander: Fureem korotoomu (フレーム·コロトーム) in the Japanese translation. The original Russian was most likely vtorom gorodom which means "the Second City."

[45] Carlander: *Terechiimu koorodomu* (テレチーム·コーロドム) in the Japanese translation. "The third city" in Russian.

[46] Iwashita: Louis Napoleon.

British reinforcements were sent to places like Barcelona and Spain, but these too were occupied by France in the end and it was all for naught. This Roman lord and the Spanish lords are currently living in France, while the lord of Barcelona fled to Brazilia.

Resenting that its territory was being reduced, Austria gathered its remaining troops and went into battle with France. In just one day, 150 000 men, including both armies, died in battle. It was a terrible war, but because the Austrian army's generals were all treacherous in nature, France escaped defeat and peace was finally made. It was decided that the king of Austria Francis the Third's daughter would be married to the French emperor and be made empress.

I recently learned that this Napoleon intends to go to war against Russia yet again, but lately he seems to have been acting docile. Alexander did agree to peace once, but I do not think he would lose easily if war broke out again.

These are all things I have now written down in order not to forget. I may however have happened to omit some smaller things or mistaken dates; I ask for your understanding in this. I have had access to no books or notes, and they are all simply things that I have memorized. Nevertheless, there is not a single word of falsehood to be found herein, and indeed just as the sun will cause clouds and fog to clear sooner or later, I believe this might shed a new light on our circumstances.

42.

If, with this document, I can lessen suspicion and dissuade people from thinking that Russia loves war, then even if I were to die here I would be happy and able to go in peace. That Russia sent an envoy[47] some years ago was purely out of a wish to form an alliance, not to make a fortune from trading. If a sound treaty were to be made then surely both of our people would benefit. Russia did thus not request permission to trade because it coveted copper or the like. The produce yielded is plentiful on both sides, but in the eastern region of Russia there is overall little; it only has plenty of high quality deer skins. And so Japan's shortage of this kind of ware became the fundamental motive behind Russia's request to Japan to conduct trade. However, perhaps because of this, Japan saw Russia as a villain and the latter was given the reply that no such thing could be permitted. The reply given to Rezanov is truly even beyond our comprehension.

[Translator's note: The "coveted copper" mentioned herein refers to Moor having heard that the Dutch are utterly greedy for Japanese copper and bring it home with them. I am told that he wrote thus to call attention to this matter. Since he had no intention of speaking only ill of Holland in this document, he thought this would suffice it seems.]

43.

Even if the eminent personages of Japan should find what I have said to be

---

[47] Iwashita: The Rezanov embassy.

suspicious, there is no reason for concern. If they send an official or two to Russia to inquire about everything, the truth will quickly be made clear. You might believe that if officials were to travel to Russia, they would be arrested and stuffed into cages like those you put animals in, and made to experience hardships, shortening their lives, but no such thing would occur. These things are not done in Russia and it is custom to only ever treat foreigners kindly. Not a single Japanese would die in prison.

44.

There is a common saying among the people in Russia: *"Pravda glaza kolet,"* meaning, "truth pricks the eyes."[48] But while this saying might apply to small-minded people, I do not think it holds true for those with a generous mind. My lord [referring to Alexander] loved horses in his youth. One time, his horse suddenly became unruly and His Imperial Majesty fell from the saddle. A peasant who was passing by just then caught the horse, and terribly angry, hit it. Leading it back to the Emperor he said, "Why would His Majesty ride a horse like this? It is no wonder you got hurt with this kind of horse. Is it not much too unwise? If His Majesty does not have any good horses, then we will present His Majesty with one even if we have to buy it. I pray His Majesty will be more careful with Himself." Alexander was grateful for this kindness and is said to have immediately replaced the horse.

[Translator's note: The common saying mentioned herein, "the truth pricks the eyes," says that if one tells nothing but the truth it might have the

---

[48] Carlander: "Правда глаза колет." Might also be translated as the more familiar, "Nothing hurts like the truth."

opposite effect of hurting people. It admonishes against situations just like the one now. However, when it comes to generous people there is no such thing, and they will be sincerely grateful like Alexander was. Moor thus meant to say that while this document may be impolite at times, he wishes for the reader to have an open mind and only look to its honesty.]

45.

Though I might as well already be facing my coffin, I have nothing left to say. Some of the matters herein may be unpleasant to hear, and I ask for your forgiveness for this. I do not wish for anything more than this, but in the event that they might be granted, I have three requests. The first one is that a copy of this document later be sent to Russia; the second that Alexei, who has met with disaster twice over, will along with my companions be spared harsh treatment; and third, that though I do not know if I will be punished or treated as a person who is ill, that even if such will be the case, these wanting words will not be thrown into the fire. These are my only wishes.

June, 1812. [The fifth month according to our calendar.] Officer of the Emperor of Russia, Moor.

A directory of the crew of the warship Diana, 25 of July, the seventh month [around the sixth month by our calendar], year 1807. [Translator's note: Since this directory lists the number of men onboard at the time of departure from the abovementioned Cronstadt, the date is given as that of the 25th of July.]

[post] Captain	[name] Vasilii	[surname] Golovnin
〃	Peter	Rickord
Lieutenant	Fyodor	Moor
〃	Ilya	Rudakov
Lieutenant	Schmiteel	Kartavchov [passed away in Kamchatka]
〃	Fuseeyo	Yakushkin
〃	Nikandor	Hiratov
Chief mate	Andrei	Harevnikov
Second mate	Vasilii	Novkii
〃	Vasilii	Sretsnii
Erekali	Bokudan	Brant
Experienced	Uhanjinmer	Skorozmov
Konstaben	Fedodo	Vavelin
Visar	Stevan	Savelev
Komisia	Elizar	Nachavinskii
Pojikibor	Igor	Iliin [passed away in Africa in 1809]
Kwardernoeshter	Igor	Savelev
〃	Ivan	Bolishakov
〃	Daniko	Labchin
Deshachnika	Ivan	Savelev [passed away in Tanani in 1809]
Harshnika	Stevan	Matershanov
Shiresare	Dmitri	Arazdobruden
Kujinyachka	Fyodor	Fyodorov
Konobachika	Ivan	Suchikov

Kupol	Alefei	Shichezurin
		[passed away in Kamchatka in 1800]
Kanoer	Ivan	Petrov
〃	Andorache	Bootov
〃	Nikihol	Kirebov
〃	Chiihan	Irenchev
Sailor	Dmirare	Shimonov
〃	Shihail	Shkaev
〃	Kirikori	Vasilev
〃	Shihiridon	Makarov
〃	Ivan	Trov
		[passed away in Kamchatka in 1809]
〃	Peter	Andretov
〃	Peter	Ivanov
		[passed away in Kamchatka in 1810]
〃	Elisei	Bruchov
〃	Grigori	Aleksandrov
〃	Ivan	Shishonov
〃	Sergei	Savelov
〃	Veshukik	Hiratora
〃	Maetro	Wolojin
〃	Mauche	Chervovin
〃	Aleksei	Ulyanov
〃	Stevan	Martemyanov
〃	Fedor	Haraharjin
〃	Semen	Krotskai

〃	Herihiu	Kirikov
		[passed away while at sea in 1809]
〃	Ilya	Sutspin
〃	Fvati	Ekseiev
〃	Nikita	Fedorov
〃	Seriv	Chimofeev
〃	Rariyon	Chimofeev
〃	Taras	Vasiliev
〃	Semen	Krarev
〃	Filip	Raromanov
〃	Ivan	Grigoriev
〃	Ivan	Suezunov
〃	Navashan	Senin
		Joined the crew while at Kamchatka.
Sailor	Vasilie	Saharov
〃	Dmitri	
		Joined the crew while in America.
Sailor	Ivan	Shyamaev
〃	Vasilii	Vasiliev
〃	Tanilo	Vovov
〃	Sergei	Aurets

The above are those who were onboard.

This concludes my translation of the document formulated and written by Moor the Russian. In the translation I have to the greatest extent possible

tried to utilize the vocabulary of the original text, but most of it was sparingly written and had an aged appearance and so in places I had to add to certain words. When the meaning of the text could not be deciphered even by adding to it, I consulted Moor and added explanatory notes in vermillion ink. The annotations in black ink sometimes found in the text did not exist in the original document, but are, as with the case of the vermillion notes, matters that I have confirmed with Moor. Since the original text also omitted the names of people in places, I added these as annotations in vermillion ink.

The speed with which Russian is spoken is unlike Japanese exceptionally fast, and so as the sentence expands in various directions there are instances where it does not make any sense in Japanese. In extreme cases, the beginning and end of the sentences are reversed. But after a while there would be parts more easily translated into Japanese and thus I translated the sentences in accordance with these. I have of course thus far translated the text in an as faithful to the original manner as possible, paying attention to the word order, but this has on the contrary made it hard to use compound words and I believe there may even be places where the meaning of the sentence is incomprehensible. With this I have now translated most of the complete work, but I am to start with unfamiliar with the Russian language and its letters, and hence, while I have translated it after being taught much by Moor, I think many discrepancies in meaning may still remain, but nevertheless I have now attempted a translation. I wrote it down and read it to Moor as well, inquiring his opinion, and he said that it was an accurate translation on the whole. And so with this I now submit this finished translation.

Fini. The fifth month of the year of the monkey.[49]

Teisuke Murakami

---

[49] Iwashita: Year 1812, or the ninth year of Bunka.

Postscript

I wonder when it was I first encountered *Moor's Report from Prison* (*Muuru Gokuchū Jyōhyō*. Hereafter referred to as "the Report"). More than 15 years have already passed since December 1999, when I first published "Regarding the First and Second Half of the Meikai University Library's *Muuru Gokuchū Jyōhyō* (Part 1)" in the *Meikai University Education, Collected Papers* Volume 11, together with my co-author, student and respected friend, Eiji Matsumoto.

As stated in this paper, the book was purchased by the Meikai University Library in 1998, which would mean that I first encountered it more than 16 years ago. I remember well that feeling when I picked up the book in the library; that gut feeling that said that this was an important piece of literature. I immediately took photos of it, and splitting the workload with Matsumoto, we deciphered the text and created a transcription. That the text contained an account of Napoleon interested me greatly.

I had originally studied the history of Napoleon's reception in Edo period Japan for my undergraduate thesis and published the paper "Biographies of Western Heros and their Reception in Japan during the Openig of the Country" based on this thesis in the *Journal of the History of Western Learning* No. 10 in 1993. Moreover, I was right in the middle of preparing for the publication of *The Napoleon Chronicles of Edo* (Chukoshinsho, 1999) at this time. Unfortunately, I was unable to incorporate the Report in this Chukoshinsho book, but I later published the continuation, part 2 and 3, of the "Regarding the First and Second Half of the Meikai University Library's *Muuru Gokuchū Jyōhyō* (Part 1)" in the *Meikai University Educa-*

tion, Collected Papers Volume 12 (2000) and 15 (2003) together with Matsumoto. I believe that I was able to include more fully the result of our research on Moor's prison report in *The Foreign Intelligence Network of the Edo Period* (Yoshikawa-kobunkan Library of History & Culture) published in 2006, the work "Regarding Historical Documents on Major Incidents in Edo Period Japan-Russia Relations" (published in *Modern Japan seen From the Eyes of Foreigners,* Takeuchi Makoto ed., Kadokawa Gakugei Publishing: 2009), and "Russian & British Overtures and Changes in Modern Japan between the 18th & Early 19th Century" (*The Cultural Situation and International Environment of Eighteenth Century Japan,* Kasaya Kazuhiko ed., Shibunkaku Publishing) .

But I still had two tasks left to do. One was the wish – no, duty – I had to publish the full text of *Moor's Report from Prison* in book format. More than anything, I wished to share the Report with the people of Russia, Europe and America who still did not know much about its existence. I would first convert the text from Edo period Japanese, closest in nature to the language of the original document, to modern Japanese and thereafter translate it into English. I was eager to have *Moor's Report from Prison* recognized since it had been overshadowed for so long by his superior Golovnin's *Narrative of my Captivity in Japan,* which contributed greatly to the development of Japanology in Europe. But this plan also meant that I would 200 years into the future be realizing the efforts of the Tenmonkata who, when in the latter half of the Edo period a Dutch copy of Golovnin's *Narrative* entered Japan through Nagasaki, noticed how its description of events differed from that of the Report. The discovery was made during the translation process, when they worked on Golovnin's *Narrative* while referring to

Moor's Report. The Tenmonkata then decided to gather copies of *Moor's Report from Prison* and put together a standardized text which they would translate into Dutch and publish in Amsterdam. I'm truly glad that I was able to make the acquaintance of my co-editor Anna Carlander (a Swedish national) on this occasion, thus making all of this reality. We have now, for the first time in 201 years, shed some light on the regret that Moor felt when he ended his own life at gun-point in 1813, and have 186 years later honored the Tenmonkata who were suppressed during the Siebold Incident (1828).

My first meeting with Anna was quite unexpected, but time and time again I have felt something inevitable behind it. It was around noon on Friday the 28th of February in 2014, during a meeting of the Koishikawa Rotary Club at the Chinzanso hotel. I had been kindly invited to this meeting by the chairman of Yushodo, Mr. Mitsuo Nitta. On Mr. Nitta's request I gave a lecture on "Little Known Facts about Perry's Arrival to Japan." A Yoneyama scholarship student, Waseda University senior Anna was also in attendance at this time. As we were seated at the same table we conversed over lunch. I learned that Anna had initially enrolled in Meikai University's School of Foreign Languages, but later transferred to Waseda University, and that she'd expressed a wish to write about something related to translation in her senior thesis. We exchanged e-mails and the talk turned to *Moor's Report from Prison.* Anna, who was also proficient in Russian, showed an interest in the work and I showed her the real *Muuru Gokuchū Jyōhyō* at the Meikai University library. It was decided that Anna would make the theme of her senior thesis the problems that might arise during the translation of such a book. It was then that the real hard work began. In the middle of my busy work schedule I would, as soon as I found a moment to

spare, translate the text bit by bit into present-day Japanese. It can probably be said that there is unlikely to be a less thankless job than interpreting Edo period Japanese translated from Russian. If we had had the original Russian text its meaning would have been made clear, but as it were, we did not. I translated the work to the best of my ability using my Edo period Japanese and poor knowledge of 19th century Western history. And somehow I was able to finish the text after the May holidays and send it to Anna. I can only guess that Anna too worked hard to translate the script into English before her graduation in September. Her knowledge of the Russian language and European history was no doubt very useful during the process. I cannot recall the number of times we met at chain restaurants in the city throughout July to work out the questions that the translation posed. It was in this manner that Anna was finally able to submit her graduation thesis, "The Misunderstood Diplomat: Midshipman Feodor Moor's role in early 19th century Japan-Russia Relations."

The thesis was reviewed by Prof. Azusa Sato, who similarly has worked at Meikai University as a part-time lecturer – here too I could not help but feel fate at work. I then presented the finished manuscript to President Yoshihiko Mitake of Yubun-Shoin and gained his ready consent to publish it. That we have now been able to do so is also much thanks to the editing skills of Mr. Takao Aoyagi. I am truly filled with a deep sense of gratitude towards everyone. I can only hope that this book will catch the eye of a great number of people.

And so to the second of the two tasks: In Golovnin's *Narrative of my Captivity in Japan,* it says that Golovnin had a tomb made for Moor, who ended his own life in Petropavlovsk-Kamchatsky. On the tombstone, the

Narrative says, is a beautiful inscription, which is also recorded in the book. However the existence of such a tombstone has yet to be confirmed. My second task is that of realizing my wish to verify its existence at the actual location. If at all possible, I would have wanted to use a picture of the tombstone as the frontispiece in the opening pages of this book. But sadly Petropavlovsk-Kamchatsky is quite a distant destination and there are no direct flights. The number of days and cost associated with such an investigation (hiring a guide, renting a car, etc.) would likely be considerable, at a rough estimate at least over 2 million yen –and thus it's sadly not a journey I can easily make reality.

But Moor was nevertheless the first ever Russian to wish to for naturalization in Japan, the first to have brought with him information on Napoleon to Japan, and while he felt such a great connection to Japan, he was also very young when he died at around 30 years of age. I would very much like to find what might be the only other proof of his existence besides the Report: his grave. I hope I will be able to visit it sometime soon.

It is with these thoughts that I now lay down my pen.

Additional note:

The above postscript was written in 2016, in preparation for the publication of this work. But as is often the case, things didn't quite go to plan. In April that year, my workplace changed from Meikai University to Toyo University, crowding my schedule and sadly taking time away from this project. At the same time, Anna graduated from Waseda University, having written her thesis on Moor, and returned to her home country to start her career. We misplaced one another's contact details and so lost touch for some years.

Director Mitake of Yubun-Shoin then also fell ill, and starting with the matter of putting the publishing house's business in order again, various unavoidable circumstances combined to make our publication plans fall through, at least for the moment.

After this, however, Director Mitake took up contact again and I managed to find Anna's Facebook, letting us reconnect. And so the publication preparations began anew in September 2020, right in the midst of the Covid-19 pandemic.

I am truly glad that we have been able to take up our work again. But in the midst of that joy there is also a sense of loss. I deeply mourn the passing of Yushodo-Shoten's late director, Mr. Mitsuo Nitta, who looked forward to this work's publication, supporting it with everything he had. May his soul rest in peace.

I would also like to take this opportunity to thank the translator and paleographer Mr. Iain Arthy, who kindly advised me on how I could find Anna on the Internet.

Last but not least, this book was made possible thanks to the help of

many. I would like to give a special thanks to Mr. Eiji Matsumoto, Mr. Yusuke Hamaguchi, and Mr. Ansei Yokota & Miss. Lisa Yokota. Your help has been priceless.

My heartfelt thanks also go to Anna, who offered to go over the translation once more after all these years, and did so without delay.

Nothing would make me happier than if this publication goes on to become a new resource for researchers of Russo-Japanese history, thus offering some consolation for Moor's late soul.

September 25, 2020

Tetsunori Iwashita

Co-editor

Iwashita Testunori

1962	Born in Nagano prefecture, Japan.
1994	Graduates from Aoyama Gakuin University's Graduate School of Literature as a History major after earning the full number of credits for the doctoral program.
1997	Becomes an instructor (later assistant professor) at Meikai University's School of Economics.
2001	Completes a Doctorate degree in History (Aoyama Gakuin University).
2005	Becomes a professor at Meikai University's School of Hospitality & Tourism.
Career	Currently works as a professor at Toyo University's Faculty of Literature as well as the University's Graduate School's graduate course in Literature.

Major works

Reflections on Oppression and Repression in East Asia (co-editor, Shumpusha Publishing), The Bloodless Capitulation of Edo (Yoshikawa Koubunkan), The Tsuyama Domain (Gendai Shokan), Disease in the Edo Period (Hokuju Shuppan), Reflections on the Systems of East Asia (co-editor, Shumpusha Publishing), A Commentary on Otsuki Bankei's "Kinkai Kikan" & 19th Century Japan's Greatest "Kinkai Kikan" and Its World (Yushodo), Reflections on East Asia's Borders (co-editor, Yubun Shoin), The Exalted Vassal of the Shogun, Takahashi Deishu (co-editor, Kyoiku Hyoron-sha), Intelligence in Japan (Yubun Shoin), A Biographical Dictionary of Foreigners in Edo Period Japan (single volume, Tokyodo Shuppan), The Earth According to the Edo Shoguns (Media Factory Shinsho), Ryoma's Understanding of the World (co-ed. with Omino Kiyoharu, Fujiwara-shoten), Intelligence Gathering in Bakumatsu Japan: Revised and Enlarged Edition (Yuzankaku Shuppan), The Forewarned Arrival of Perry & the Bakumatsu's Intelligence War (Yosen-sha), Tokugawa Yoshinobu – The Man and the Age He Lived in (writer-editor, Iwata-shoin), Edo Information Theory (Hokuju Shuppan), Intelligence Gathering in Bakumatsu Japan (Yuzankaku Shuppan), Influential People & the Medicines of Edo (Hokuju Shuppan), Foreign Intelligence in Modern Japan (co-ed. with Maehira Fusaaki, Iwata-shoin).

Anna Linnea Carlander

1989	Born in Örnsköldsvik, Sweden.
2009	Moves to Tokyo, Japan to study the Japanese language.
2012	Becomes a Rotary Yoneyama Memorial Foundation Fellow. Rotary club: Tokyo Koishikawa Rotary Club.
2014	Graduates from Waseda University School of International Liberal Studies with a Bachelorate of Arts in International Liberal Studies (early graduation).
	Graduates as an "Outstanding Achiever." Graduation thesis is chosen as an "Excellent Senior Thesis."
	Thesis title: "The Misunderstood Diplomat: Midshipman Feodor Moor's role in early 19th century Japan-Russia Relations."

Career

Began working as a freelance translator of Japanese, English and Swedish in 2012 while still living and studying in Tokyo. Discovers the world of literary agencies in 2013 and joins the Tokyo-based agency Cork, Inc. as a translator, interpreter and editor. Moves to Stockholm, Sweden in 2014 after graduating from Waseda University, and founds the translation agency Compass Translations. Joins Northern Europe's leading literary agency, Salomonsson Agency, in 2015 and works there to date.

ロシア海軍少尉
ムールの苦悩

2021年7月21日印刷
2021年7月30日発行

著　者　岩下哲典
　　　　アンナ リネア・カーランデル
装　幀　鬼武健太郎
発行者　三武義彦
発行所　株式会社右文書院
　　　　東京都千代田区神田駿河台1-5-6 ／郵便番号101-0062
　　　　tel. 03-3292-0460　fax. 03-3292-0424
　　　　http://www.yubun-shoin.co.jp/
　　　　mail@yubun-shoin.co.jp

印刷・製本　株式会社文化印刷

ISBN978-4-8421-0819-3　C0020

編者紹介

岩下哲典（いわした・てつのり）

1962年	長野県に生まれる。
1994年	青山学院大学大学院文学研究科史学専攻博士後期課程満期退学。
1997年	明海大学経済学部専任講師（のち助教授）。
2001年	博士（歴史学、青山学院大学）
2005年	明海大学ホスピタリティ・ツーリズム学部教授。
現　在	東洋大学文学部教授（大学院文学研究科教授兼担）

主な著作

『東アジアの弾圧・抑圧を考える』（共編著、春風社）『江戸無血開城』（吉川弘文館）、『病とむきあう江戸時代』（北樹出版）、『津山藩』（現代書館）、『東アジアの秩序を考える』（共編著、春風社）『解説　大槻磐渓「金海奇観」と19世紀の日本――「金海奇観」とその世界――』（雄松堂書店）、『東アジアのボーダーを考える』（共編著、右文書院）、『高邁なる幕臣　高橋泥舟』（編著、教育評論社）、『日本のインテリジェンス』（右文書院）、『江戸時代来日外国人人名辞典』（単編、東京堂出版）、『江戸将軍が見た地球』（メディアファクトリー新書）、『龍馬の世界認識』（藤原書店、小美濃清明氏と共編）、『［改訂増補版］幕末日本の情報活動』（雄山閣出版）、『予告されていたペリー来航と幕末情報戦争』（洋泉社）、『徳川慶喜　その人と時代』（岩田書院、編著）、『江戸情報論』（北樹出版）、『幕末日本の情報活動』（雄山閣出版）、『権力者と江戸のくすり』（北樹出版）、『近世日本の情報活動』（岩田書院、真栄平房昭氏と共編）。

Carlander, Anna Linnea（カーランデル・アンナ　リネア）

1989年	スウェーデンのÖrnsköldsvik市（エルンシェルツビク市）に生まれる。
2009年	語学留学のため来日する。
2012年	公益財団法人ロータリー米山記念奨学生に選ばれる。
	世話クラブ：東京小石川ロータリークラブ
2012年	日本語・英語・スウェーデン語のフリーランス翻訳者として働き始める。
2013年	文学エージェンシーの世界を発見し、東京を拠点とするエージェンシー Cork, Incにて翻訳者・通訳者・編集者として加わる。
2014年	早稲田大学国際教養学部学士学位取得（特別制度早期卒業）
	卒業の際「Outstanding Achiever」（優れた業績を残した者）に選ばれる。
	卒業の際に卒業論文は「優秀作品」に選ばれる。
	卒業論文タイトル：「The Misunderstood Diplomat: Midshipman Feodor Moor's role in early 19th century Japan-Russia Relations」（誤解された外交官：海軍士官フョードル・ムールが19世紀初頭の日蘭関係において果たした役割）

早稲田大学卒業後、スウェーデンのストックホルムに移り、翻訳会社Compass Translationsを設立。
2015年に北ヨーロッパ最大の文学エージェンシーであるSalomonsson Agencyに加わる。